BACK FROM THE BARDO
SECOND EDITION
Includes the Mind of Frank Rosseus

JAMES CAGE

Back From the Bardo Second Edition
Includes the Mind of Frank Rosseus
James Cage

Special Revised Edition May, 2014
ISBN-13: 978-1484884201
ISBN-10: 1484884205

Copyright can be found in the Library of Congress
Cataloging Publication Data
Cage, James.

Book Cover Design:
Between Heaven & Hell by Alan Mahood
Copyright © 2011 Alan Mahood
C-ART Gallery, Newport Beach, CA

Printed by CreateSpace an Amazon Company

Publication History
Back From the Bardo
Three Short Stories
By James Cage
Copyright © 2006 by James Cage
Original Paperback Edition
Published by BookSurge Publishers 2006
ISBN: 1-4196-2994-8

Holding the Bricks
By James Cage
Work of Fiction
Copyright © 1987 by James Cage
First Published on the Web by Lucky Statistics 2000

Astral Andy and the Funny Bear
By James Cage
Work of Fiction
Copyright © 2000 by James Cage
First Published on the Web by Lucky Statistics 2000

Germ Spreaders on a Train
By James Cage
Work of Fiction
Copyright © 2006 by James Cage
Published as the third section of Back from the Bardo, in Paperback
By BookSurge Publishers 2006

The Mind of Frank Rosseus
By James Cage
Work of Fiction
Copyright © 2012 by James Cage
First Published as an E-Book
By Smashwords.com December, 2012
ISBN: 9781301107230

James Cage

BACK FROM THE BARDO
Second Edition
Includes
The Mind of Frank Rosseus

Contents

PROLOGUE

Prayer to St. Michael the Archangel

O Glorious Prince of the heavenly host, St. Michael the Archangel, defend us in the battle and in the terrible warfare that we are waging against the principalities and powers, against the rulers of this world of darkness, against evil spirits. Come to the aid of man, whom Almighty God created immortal, made in His own image and likeness, and redeemed at a great price from the tyranny of Satan.

James Cage

Photo: The Fire-Eater
Courtesy V.J. DiGiovanni
Guadalajara, Jalisco Mexico 1977

Book I: HOLDING THE BRICKS

July, 1976

It is the middle of the rainy season, a hot, muggy, July Saturday night in Guadalajara, Mexico. As I stroll along Avenida Mungia, I listen to meat broiling on a taco cart. Written by a prankster, *"Carne de Perro,"* is scribbled on the side of this cart. Nonetheless, there are a number of customers enjoying the tacos.

I just left the Teatro Reforma having viewed a very funny Italian film starring Ugo Tognazzi. The name of the film with Spanish subtitles is called *Venga a Tomar Una Taza de Cafe con Nosotros*. I think the Mexicans can understand Italian fairly well.

From inside a Volkswagen, a voice shouts, "Jaime, Jaime." It's Tom and I'm glad to see him. He pulls the car next to me, flips open the door and I jump in.

Tom is twenty-eight years old, dark hair, brown eyes. He speaks fluent Spanish. He is an American medical student, studying in Guadalajara. He pays for his education by dealing marijuana. Most Americans are home for summer vacation. However, I am stuck in Mexico, repeating examinations. Tom is here making drug deals.

Tom says, "What do you know about cocaine, Jaime?"

"Not too much," I answer.

Tom drives the car straight through Avenida La Paz, spins it around the Fire-Eater in the middle of the road, cuts a right turn then zigzags down side streets until we reach his house.

Tom lives on a quiet street, located in a community behind the shopping mall, Plaza del Sol. His newly built home has chopped glass cemented into the roof with iron bars covering the windows. He parks his car in the driveway and we go inside.

"Jaime, I have something to show you." Tom disappears into his bedroom, while I inspect the Indian rug hanging from the wall. A few minutes later he reappears with a large Ricamesa shopping bag and pulls out two white bricks and says, "Each brick is ninety percent pure cocaine. They weigh one kilo per piece and cost ten grand each. Do you have twenty thousand dollars Jaime?"

"I don't have that kind of money. Hmm, well maybe I know someone who does." Then I add, "Hey Tom, how are you going to get that stuff across the border?"

Tom responds, "Look, here in Mexico the price of this coke is twenty thousand. Once it is on the USA side of the border, it goes for forty or fifty thousand dollars wholesale. If you cut this stuff and deal it, the profit can be much more, maybe even two hundred thousand bucks."

"Wow," I say, as he hands me a can of Tecate beer.

"Ok Jaime, who's your friend with the money?"

"You know him, last summer he lived in the apartment next to me. He is a kid from Ohio, named Rob Loesser. He wasn't here long. Rob studied Spanish for a few months, and then went back to the states."

Tom says, "I remember him, you took him to the whorehouses because he was afraid to go there by himself. Am I right?"

"Yes, that's the guy."

"Look Jaime, I want you to do me a favor. Keep these bricks for me until Thursday. I am driving to Puerto Vallarta tonight to look into another deal."

"Why me," I ask.

"Because I know you won't do the drugs. Tom smiles, I can trust you."

Tom drops me off at Minerva Circle in the center of town. I walk a few blocks to my apartment building, carrying the bricks in the Ricamesa shopping bag. Once inside the apartment, I lock my door and place the bricks into a closet. I also lock the closet. I go to bed, slightly disturbed.

Thursday finally comes. I wait all day and then go to Tom's house. There is no Tom. While driving from Guadalajara to Puerto Vallarta, it is a common occurrence for Mexicans, American tourists and students to fly their cars off the mountains. The tortuous highway that connects Guadalajara to mountain town of Tepic, than goes down through the jungle into Puerto Vallarta.

I search the newspapers *El Occidental*, *El Informador*, and the *English Language News* for accident reports. There are many accidents, but none involve a Tom Jenner or a 1970 brown Volkswagen Beetle with California plates.

August, 1976

It is now the first Monday in August. The semester at the university begins and the contingent of American students returns for classes. Tom has been missing three weeks. A couple of students, one from Minnesota, the other from Texas ask me about Tom's whereabouts.

I say, "I haven't seen him in school today." These two guys proceed to ask others about Tom. I figure they are worrying about their marijuana source.

The cocaine traffic in Guadalajara is controlled by a gang of vicious young thugs from Culiacan, a city north of Mazatlan, on Mexico's west coast. These gangsters know where every brick of cocaine is from Acapulco to Nogales. Tom would never have two kilos of pure coke without paying them first. So, Tom is gone and I've been left holding the bricks beneath the watchful, unseen eye of the Mexican Mafia.

I continue to go to school every day, study as well as I can and keep to a normal schedule. Workouts at the gym, dinner and movies are part of my activities. Sometimes I get a girl from downtown. As the weeks pass by, my stomach is upset, I have problems sleeping and I am losing weight.

October, 1976

It is ten o'clock, Saturday evening, the ninth of October. I will be unable to sleep. I get into my car and drive down Avenida Vallarta through Avenida Juarez into the busy and heavily trafficked center of the city. I continue to drive onto Avenida Javier Mina to the red light district.

I park the car on a side street and walk to a building with a red light dangling from the top of the doorway. I press the buzzer. A small window opens and an eye peers through it. The man opens the door. I walk in and go up a flight of stairs.

It is smoky and crowded inside the whorehouse. There are waiters, bouncers, girls and customers. There are no Americans in this place, only Mexican males, young and old. I am the only American in the house. Olivia Newton John sings in English on the radio, "Come on over put a smile on my face."

I stand at the large bar in the middle of the main room. A waiter comes over and says, "*Que pasa?*"

I ask, "*Ester esta aqui?*"

"*Si.*"

The waiter calls a girl over. She leaves the room to go find Ester. He says, "*Una toma?*"

"*Una cerveza.*"

The waiter brings me a bottle of Superior Beer. I hand him ten pesos and give him another ten pesos tip. I take a swig of beer from the bottle.

I feel a tap on my shoulder. Ester is behind me. I have known Ester for three years. She is twenty-six years old, five feet two inches tall, dark hair, dark eyes, dark skin, very pretty and well built. She speaks and understands English. However, inside the whorehouse I speak to her only in Spanish.

"*Por toda la noche.*"

She says, "*Un momento Jaime. Ya me voy a conseguir mi chaqueta.*"

I wait a second. Linda Ronstadt sings in English on the radio, "You're no good, baby you're no good."

Outside the house, Ester and I walk down the street to my car. I open the car door for her, she gets in and we drive to a motel.

Inside the motel room, Ester and I drink a couple of beers. She turns the radio on and Mexican music plays softly. "*Ya no me cantes cigarra. Que acabe tu sonsonete.*"

Ester kicks off her shoes and sits on the bed. She sips the beer then places the bottle down on the night table. She lights a Baronet cigarette and gives it to me. She then lights one up for herself.

She says, "Jaime, you have lost weight."

I answer, "Yes, a little. How have you been Ester?"

"More or less well. How come you have not called me?"

"I have had a lot to study at school. Ester, I am going to leave Mexico and I am not coming back."

"You always come back, Jaime."

"Not this time."

James Cage

Ester touches me. We go to bed.

It is Monday afternoon, the eleventh of October. The air is cooler and the rainy season has ended. I am standing inside the school administration building, located in sector Lomas Del Valle, an upscale area of Guadalajara. An attractive, young Mexican woman is busy looking through a file cabinet. After a few minutes of reading, she shuts the cabinet drawer, turns and walks to the counter in front of me. She states softly, "Senor Thomas Jenner has taken a leave of absence from school and will resume studies in January." She smiles, "Jaime, when are you taking me to dinner again?"

"Next week, y muchas gracias," I answer. She smells of nice perfume. I like this girl. I exit.

Early the next morning, after receiving the news that Tom has taken a leave of absence, I drive my car to Servicio Jose Vallarta. The car needs an oil change, tune up and brake job. Then I hail a taxi and journey to the city of Tlaquepaque, a downscale suburb of Guadalajara. There is an area in this town of artisans where one can have specific items made to order by skilled craftsmen. I shop around, pick up some souvenirs, drink a Corona and take a cab home.

The bricks of cocaine have been in my closest untouched for three months. I close the shades to my windows, dead bolt my door, take the bricks out of the Ricamesa shopping bag and place them on a clean table. Using a hammer and screwdriver, I chop one brick into a large, grainy pile. I divide this pile into six smaller lumps. I wrap the individual lumps inside cellophane, sponge and cotton, covering each with a large sock. I repeat the process with the second brick. To protect the souvenirs I purchased in Tlaquepaque, I also cover these items with cotton, sponge and a heavy brown sweater. I pack the socks and sweater into a heavy, duty gym bag. The few items of clothing I own are packed into two medium sized suitcases. Textbooks and notebooks are placed inside two cardboard cartons. It is now late afternoon. I double check my apartment and go to pick up my car.

Jose, at Servicio Jose Vallarta, is an excellent mechanic who can fix anything inside or outside a car. He charges fair rates and gives rapid service. He has completed the repairs on my red 1970 Chevy Malibu with Texas plates. Jose says, "*Donde vas, Jaime?*"

"*Quien sabe*," I answer.

It is 5 AM, Wednesday, the thirteenth of October. As I drive through the eastern mountains, I slow the car and turn to see the lights of Guadalajara in the valley behind me. I take a gulp from a can of Tecate and wash down a Lomotil to ease my stomach for the six hundred fifty miles ride ahead. After two hours of rough, mountain driving, I stop for gas at the Pemex station, in the not so hot town of Tabasco. The peasants in Tabasco look like movie extras in films about Emiliano Zapata. I pass them by as they wait at the bus stop.

I am back on Highway 54 North going out from the mountains. When I get to Zacatecas, I pop a Fleetwood Mac tape into a Panasonic recorder. I just listen to the music and follow the road ahead. The next gas stop is Villa de Cos where the Mexican army checks vehicles going south for guns and other contraband. They don't bother to check vehicles driving north.

The next two hundred fifty miles are two lanes highway across the Mexican desert to Saltillo. This is a relatively safe journey in daylight. Trucks and buses are visible for hundreds of yards. It is simple to pass or slow down. The desert air in October is clear and the temperature is only in the low eighty's at the warmest. The desert smells good. It is a nice ride.

Through Saltillo, I motor into the congested traffic of the industrial city of Monterrey. I stop for gas and continue to drive toward the American frontier. Ten miles from the border, I am stopped by the Mexican Federales. They check my car papers, find them to be in order and I continue onward. Thus, I have been granted unmolested passage through Mexico by the drug Mafia.

On the United States side of the border at Laredo, Texas, my car idles in the inspection lane. I open a bottle of Coke and sip from it. I watch customs agents thoroughly search a Ford van in the opposite lane.

Another customs agent comes to check my car. He says in a heavily accented West Texas drawl, "License and registration, please."

I hand him my Texas documents.

He says, "Remove your key and get out of the car, please."

I get out of the car, drinking my soda.

The custom agent orders, "Open your trunk. Do you have anything to declare, fruits or vegetables?"

I answer, "I have nothing to declare."

The customs agent does a half-assed job checking the baggage in the car trunk. He does not open the luggage. He does not even bother to check the gym bag inside the car.

Then he asks, "When was the last time you were in Texas?
"Six months ago."

"Do you have any food from Mexico?"

"Just this Coke," I answer.

"Get the fuck out of here, wise-ass."

I get back in my car and get the fuck out of there.

The entire road trip has taken thirteen hours. I register for a room at the Grand Hotel in Laredo. Once in the room, I vomit before crawling into bed. I have a nightmare.

Flashback 1966

It is 1966. I am sixteen or seventeen years old. I am in my Uncle Jerry's bar and grill in Greenpoint, Brooklyn, New York. I have just cleaned the place up and drink a glass of milk in the kitchen. My uncle drinks a cup of black coffee. It is the middle of the night. The wall clock shows 3:00 o'clock.

The door to the bar is open and two large men walk in. My uncle goes into the barroom. He recognizes the men. He says, "Hey guys, what's up?"

The two men draw revolvers with silencers and shoot at Uncle Jerry. Uncle Jerry quickly dives behind the bar. As the two men move around the side of the bar to kill him, I enter the room from the kitchen back entrance. The men hear me and turn. I unload into them at close range, double barreled, sawoffed twelve gauge shotgun shells. The shotgun blasts are not so loud. The two men drop. I stand motionless and stare at the dead men. I have blown their heads off.

Uncle Jerry comes from around the bar. He has been shot, there is blood dripping from his right shoulder. With his good left hand, he grabs the shotgun from me.

He says, "Go home and don't ever say a word about this to anyone. I will take care of everything. Thanks Jimmy."

Back to Present

It is Thursday, October 14. 1976. I awake from my nightmare, shaking. I jump into the shower, dry myself and inspect my body in the full length bathroom mirror. I have lost at least fifteen pounds since July. I am very thin. About the same weight I was ten years ago.

I continue my journey, drive up Highway 35 North and pull into a McDonald's at Austin, Texas.

I enter the hamburger restaurant. There are three very pretty teenaged girls in blue jeans and boots sitting in a booth enjoying their meal. They are having a happy, gleeful conversation. One of the girls, a tall, good looking blonde has an exceptionally beautiful pair of well-endowed breasts. She turns her head and smiles at me. I silently smile at her. I exit the restaurant. I will have the food in my car.

I turn on the radio. Roy Orbison sings, "I feel so bad, I've got a worried mind."

Texas is cowboys and trucks, country music and beer, shotguns and pretty women. I love Texas. I feel secure here.

When I finish my meal I go to the phone booth, outside McDonald's. I telephone Rob Loesser in Ohio.

"Hello, is Rob there?" I say to the guy who answers the phone, who I know to be Rob.

"Yes, this is he. Who is this?"

"It's me, your buddy from the Guad," I respond.

"Hey Jaime, how ya doin?" he answers excitedly.

I deposit some more change into the telephone and say. "Look, Rob, I got some stuff you may be interested in. It is rather expensive. The cost is negotiable. Have you been in

James Cage

contact with Tom? You understand what I am talking about, don't you?"

"Yeah, I've been waiting to hear from you for a long time," Rob answers. I can hear him light a cigarette, as he slowly says, "Where can we meet?"

I say, "Little Rock, Arkansas, the Ramada Inn, it is on Highway 30 West. Check in before 2 PM on Saturday." I hang up the phone because I am running out of change.

Rob is a rich young man. He lives from a trust fund, given to him by his grandfather. He told me that he receives one hundred thousand per year. He is tall and blond. He is a drug dealer. He checked out the medical school and the drugs in Mexico. He chose the drugs. Rob would have to do his drug dealing in the United States because the Mexicans won't deal with a blondie like Rob. They will only deal with a macho, like Tom.

I arrive in Little Rock at noon on Saturday, the sixteenth of October. I park my car one half mile from the Ramada Inn and call the hotel from a phone booth. I ask for Mr. Loesser. The switchboard connects us and Rob says, "Come on over, I am in room 214."

I walk over to the hotel carrying the gym bag. I enter the Ramada Inn through a side entrance. I have stayed at this hotel on three separate occasions. It is easy for me to find room 214. I knock at the door. Rob opens the door and I walk into the room. Tom Jenner sits on the bed, calmly watching television. There is a presidential campaign commercial on the television and I say, "Who is this guy, Jimmy Carter?"

Tom answers, "You are not surprised to see me are you, Jaime?"

I say, "You set me up to carry this stuff across the border. I figured that out when I found you had taken a leave of absence for the semester. Before that I thought you were killed."

Then Tom says, "You were the only guy who could carry that coke across the border and get away with it. Rob and I were certain you would make it. My Mexican friends wouldn't bother you. It was US customs that you had to clear and you did."

I respond. "Well, I wasn't so sure. I know the cocaine is odorless but just in case, I wrapped it in cellophane, cotton and sponge. There weren't any dogs at US customs." I then open the gym bag and place twelve socks on one of the beds.

Rob hands me four stacks of bills. There are twenty-five, one hundred dollar bills in each stack. I think four times twenty-five times one hundred equals ten thousand dollars.

Tom says, "The cocaine cost twenty grand in Mexico. This ten thousand is for you, Jaime. The entire investment equals thirty thousand dollars." He repeats, "You just made yourself ten grand, Jaime."

I answer, "Good enough." But I think the cocaine is worth a lot more than thirty grand on the USA side of the border. Tom had told me months earlier that this amount of cocaine is worth forty to fifty thousand dollars wholesale once it is inside the United States.

In good spirits, Rob and Tom unravel the socks. They begin to weigh the coke on a small grocery store scale. I am watching them. They say that they will cut the stuff and distribute it in Chicago. Tom tells me, "This cocaine stepped on a few times can be worth at least a quarter million dollars on the street."

I open my gym bag again. "Thud, thud," speaks the gun. Two bullets rip into Tom's skull. "Pop, pop," Rob's eyes are bloody holes. The last two bullets thud into the hearts of Tom and Rob. That completes the double murder.

I make a mental note that the silencer made by the artesian in Tlaquepaque caused a somewhat louder pop, thud sound than I expected. The .38 caliber long barrel revolver is recommended for its accuracy. It worked rather well.

I put the gun and money inside the gym bag and take a final look at the white powder cocaine and two bloody bodies lying on the floor. I close the door to room 214. I vacate the Ramada Inn from the opposite side of the building carrying the gym bag in my left hand.

On the road again, I reach the Mississippi River at Memphis, Tennessee. I drive down to the riverbank and throw the gun and silencer into the murky water. I decide to drive to New

York. Maybe I'll visit some relatives. Back on the interstate highway, I turn the radio on. The announcer states, "The New York Yankees and the Cincinnati Reds are playing in the World Series tomorrow."

"Well," I speak aloud, "I wonder how that will turn out?"

Book II: ASTRAL ANDY AND THE FUNNY BEAR

Rome, Italy July 4, 1980

My cousin Nicky and I are drinking espresso while relaxing inside, the outside cafe of the Excelsior Hotel on the Via Veneto in Rome, Italy. It is the Fourth of July 1980, a very warm evening. Earlier in the afternoon the communists held a small demonstration in front of the American Embassy. Tonight, we sit and watch the pretty Italian girls walk by. The girls wear light summer dresses, blouses, have bare, shaved legs and wear sandals.

Nicky says, "The girls don't shave their armpits." Then he says, "Northern Italians say Africa starts south of Rome."

Well, tonight we feel the hot African breeze blowing through us.

More people pass by the café and suddenly I see him, the Funny Bear. He has changed somewhat. He must be over sixty years old. His curly, thick, dark, brown hair has become white. He looks strong as a grizzly bear. He stands six feet four inches tall and weighs two hundred thirty pounds of solid muscle. He has maintained a flat stomach. The lady with him is a mature young woman, early thirties. She is a knockout: flawless skin, blue eyes, dirty blond hair and beautiful legs. She is tall, five feet eight or five nine. Perhaps she is a model or maybe an actress. Even though he has not looked in my direction, I know The Bear sees me. Nicky takes a long, long stare at the young lady.

"What a beautiful woman, how old do you think she is?"

"A couple of years older than I am," I respond.

Suddenly, The Bear turns around, looks at me. He grins. I smile silently and nod back. The Funny Bear and the pretty lady walk away. I order two shots of Galliano for my cousin and me.

Nicky is taking an Italian vacation before he begins his final year of medical school in the United States. I am accompanying him. After drinking the whiskey, we return to the Hotel Quattro Fontani. It is a second-class hotel. We have a small room without air conditioning. Nicky goes to sleep.

I open a composition book and write the following:

Mexico, July 4, 1971

Stella Maris Hotel, Mexico City, July 4, 1971. I am in the dining room having dinner: steak, beans and salad. The book I am reading is *The Third Eye* by T. Lobsang Rampa. A really big man and a brown skinned, well-built Mexican girl are seated at the table across from me. I think. What a fine looking Mexican girl she is.

The big man gets up, walks over to my table and says, "Are you into astral projection?"

"No," I answer. "I am interested in comparative religions. I am not sure the author of this book is a Tibetan monk as stated."

"Why is that," says the big man.

"Because the author mentions God and Buddhists do not believe in an all-powerful God."

The big man asks, "Do you believe, the author, Rampa can astrally project himself to wherever he wishes?"

I respond, "Maybe he can, but I really don't know anything about astral projection."

Next he reaches out an extra-large hairy hand, "My name is George Foster."

"My name is Andy."

"Andy, are you on a Mexican holiday?"

"Yes," I answer.

"Well, sit and have dinner with Marta and me instead of being alone."

"No thanks, I'm finished with dinner."

"Then have an after dinner drink and coffee with us," says George.

Feeling a bit lonely, I accept the offer. I drink black coffee with George and his companion, Marta. I tell him my name is Andrew Jackson Como. I wanted to say Stonewall Jackson or Perry Como but it came out, Andrew Jackson Como.

George has a British accent. After some conversation, he invites me to accompany him to a gun club at 10 AM tomorrow morning. I think this is strange.

"George, I have not shot a gun since I was seventeen years old."

"About five years ago?" He questions.

"Yes, exactly," I answer.

George says that he can teach me to shoot targets. He asks if the glasses I wear are for reading or do I need them all the time.

I say, "I am near sighted and need glasses all the time but I can read without them."

"That's fine," he answers.

The following morning at the gun club, George teaches me how to use a Remington model 40X, single shot, .22-caliber rifle. When I was a teenager, my friends took me to a target range. They taught me how to shoot a target rifle similar to this one. This morning George shows me how to sight the target, point the weapon and squeeze the trigger. After four shots, I finally hit a bull's eye on the fifth try at 100 meters.

George takes me to a local restaurant for lunch and begins to ask me questions.

"Are you a draft dodger Andy?"

"No," I answer. "I have a high draft lottery number. I don't think I will be drafted."

George wants to know more about me. So I tell him honestly. "I graduated from college in June. If I were drafted I would go into the army without hesitation but I am not the volunteer type. I don't want some Sergeant yelling orders at me all day. I have no political points of view concerning the war in Vietnam."

George keeps asking questions. He says, "Do you enjoy traveling alone in Mexico?"

"Yes, I can go where I want, when I want. I may visit the Mayan ruins in southern Mexico and in Tikal, Guatemala. Then I shall go home."

"Where is your home?"

I tell George, "I live with my grandmother and my cousin Nicky in New York City."

"Do you have a job, Andy?"

"When I get back home, I'll look for a job as a general elementary school teacher or a high school biology teacher. However, I would like to stay in Mexico for a semester to study Spanish at UNAM. You can see the university over there." I point my finger toward the school.

He says, "Would you like to make a decent amount of money."

"Depends on the type of work involved," I respond.

George answers, "You can be a private teacher for a couple of children. But the job entails that you also know how to protect them? I can personally teach you how to use a gun. My friends can teach you martial arts and other methods of protection."

"You mean I would also be a bodyguard."

"Yes."

"How much money would I be paid?" I question.

"Twenty thousand dollars," says George.

"When can I start?"

"It will take eight to ten weeks to train you as a bodyguard."

"I cannot tell my grandmother, I have a job as a bodyguard."

"No of course not, you can tell her that you are taking a two months course in Spanish. I can arrange a post office box for you here, in Mexico City. I can have your letters postmarked from Mexico City and have letters from your family brought to you at my ranch in Guatemala."

I say, "Guatemala?"

George says, "You wanted to go see the Mayan ruins in Tikal, my place is better. If you do not like the training you can leave. Or, if I feel you don't have the ability to perform the job, I shall discharge you. Here is two thousand dollars." He hands me an envelope with cash inside.

George continues, "I shall give you eight thousand dollars at the end of your training and another ten thousand dollars when the job is completed. All expenses, travel and living are covered."

I did not have to think about this. Twenty thousand dollars is a fortune to me. "Ok, I'll do it but if this does not work out, do I keep the two thousand dollars?"

"Yes, you keep the two thousand and I shall pay for your plane ticket home," answers George.

"What happens if I get killed when I am working as a bodyguard?"

George says, "Our employers will send your grandmother a check from a life insurance company in the amount of twenty thousand dollars. She will get a document stating you died in an accident and your body was cremated."

"Ok," I answer.

I figure George has been observing me at the hotel. I arrived two days ago. The only things I have done since arriving in Mexico were to visit the National Autonomous University of Mexico (UNAM) and go to a movie.

I saw the film *Ulysses* starring Kirk Douglas. It was dubbed in Italian. Or maybe it was originally made in Italian and dubbed in English. I don't know. I am sure George knows that Andrew Jackson Como is not my real name.

Arrangements are made to leave for Guatemala in two days. George asks me for my passport. He says he will supply me with another passport and I will get my original back when the training period is over. I give the passport to him.

George asks, "Do you want Andrew Jackson Como on the new passport?"

I say, "Whatever name you want, put on it."

My new passport is British. My name is James Andrews. My place of birth is Toronto, Canada. I am one year older. The picture is exactly the same as the original passport picture. I have a visa for Guatemala. The plane ticket is Mexicana Airlines one way to Guatemala City.

James Cage

Guatemala

I arrive with George and Marta at La Aurora Airport in Guatemala City. Two guys pick us up in a large Jeep. Luke Two is one guy. He is around thirty years old. Luke is thin, wiry and slightly oriental looking. He says that he is a Filipino Greek. The other guy is a black dude. His name is Johnny Walker. John is as tall as George but thinner. John is young looking but close to forty years old.

George points toward me and says, "This is Jaime."

We drive onto the main road. The city has low buildings and I don't get a good view. The countryside is hilly with banana and coffee plantations. The colors of the mountains are green and dark brown.

We pass through the gates of a ranch. Above the entry gate are the words SAMBALANGA RANCH. I shall be staying here. The size of the ranch is one hundred hectares or two hundred forty acres. The location is twenty kilometers northeast from central Guatemala City. It rains every day. It is warm and humid. There are horses, cows, barns, corrals and storage silos. There are fields of corn, coffee and fruits. There is an outside shooting range with stationary targets.

A large building with a small gym, meeting room and dining hall is located a few meters east from the main ranch house. There is a wood burning stove in the kitchen of the dining hall.

The main ranch house is in the middle of the estate. There is a new electrical system and telephone service is provided. George Foster, the owner of the estate, lives in the main house with his girlfriend Marta. She goes back and forth to Mexico City every two weeks. She brings back small personal items including mail posted to Mexico City. At times George uses a short wave radio for communications instead of the telephone.

A motel type building with a water tower is the next building east of the dining hall. I live alone in one of the motel rooms. The contents of each room are exactly the same: one single bed, a desk, chair, electric lamp, kerosene lamp and bottled water. The electricity does not always work and I use the kerosene lamp to read in the evening. I have a private bathroom with a shower. The hot water never gets hot. Maids change the towels every day and the bed sheets once a week. Luke Two and Johnny Walker live in the rooms on each side of me. Five other men live in the motel. Three are young men: Alan Sinclair, his brother Paolo (Paul) Sinclair and Marcos diRandi. There are two older men who are instructors. They are The Colonel and The Major. I assume they are all advanced bodyguards. A better word is mercenaries. I am the only novice.

At the opposite end of the finca, there are Guatemalan workers living on the estate in a similar motel type building. The workers call George, "Oso Sonrisa," or Grinning Bear. My translation is Funny Bear.

September, 1971

It is Thursday, the second of September, 1971. I have been on this ranch for nine weeks. George personally trained me. He taught me to use the Remington 40x, .22-caliber target rifle. He showed me how to shoot an AK47 machine gun, with thirty rounds in the magazine. George told me to use the machine gun as a semi-automatic weapon and squeeze the shots one at a time. He also taught me how to shoot a single shot sniper rifle with scope. This weapon had no markings on it.

He said, "This sniper rifle is a Russian Dragunov. The cartridge is 7.62mm by 54. It is longer than the cartridge used in the AK47 machine gun, which is 7.62mm by 39.

George the Bear taught me to adjust the scope on the sniper rifle starting at twenty-five meters and ending at three hundred meters. If I did not hit the target dead on at one hundred meters, I had to adjust by four clicks per inch (2.54 centimeters) to the right or left when I missed the bull's eye. He said any real shooting I may do, would be under two hundred meters or around two hundred yards at maximum. The scope on the sniper rifle made it easy to hit a bull's eye after a small adjustment. George also taught me to shoot a Smith and Wesson .38 caliber, long barrel policemen's special. George carried a Colt Model 1911, Commander .45 caliber semi-automatic pistol with seven rounds in the magazine.

George taught me how to shoot the pistol but I did not get one for myself.

During the summer, all the young mercenaries: Alan, Paolo, Marcos and I would meet in the gym for physical training. We would spend two hours each day learning boxing, judo and karate techniques. Some of the street fighting, methods were extremely vicious. Johnny Walker was the physical training instructor. Luke Two was the instructor for knife fighting. The Major was our Spanish instructor and The Colonel taught us how to use a ham radio.

Tonight George calls me into his office. He opens the dossier of my life and proceeds to read it to me.

"You were raised in New Jersey and New York. You graduated college in Jersey City this past June. You were an average student. Your father died of cancer in 1965. Your mother, her brother and his wife died in an automobile accident on the New Jersey Turnpike in 1968. Now you live with your Grandmother and your younger cousin Nicky in a Manhattan apartment complex located at First Avenue and East Fifteenth Street. It was your cousin Nicky's parents that were killed in the accident with your mother. Your Grandmother is an elementary school teacher and your cousin Nicky is a high school student. You have two close friends. One enlisted in the Navy and the other enlisted in the Marines. You like girls but never had a steady girlfriend. You are a loner by nature. You have one uncle from your mother's side that lives in California. He is a very successful businessman. You have another uncle from your father's side of the family. He lives in Brooklyn where he owns a bar. He is connected to organized crime. He served two years for a double manslaughter from 1967 through 1969.

I say, "Well George, you know all about me."

George says, "I am going to show you a film. Atrocities were committed against innocent peasants. The men responsible for these murders are in Guatemala."

Today is Friday, the third of September. George, John, Luke and I are going on a road trip. George and I travel in one Jeep while Luke and John follow us in another Jeep. An AK47 with two fully loaded magazines are in each Jeep. John, Luke and I have sniper rifles with six jacketed hollow point rounds each. These bullets have some lead taken out of the middle. The machine gun rounds are full metal jacket, solid lead filling the metal cartridge. George carries his Colt 45. The weapons are covered with large heavy bags.

We cross the Motagua River north of the town of Zacapa. We go deeper into the jungle and stop the Jeeps. We walk for a while. Two hundred meters below, is a clear area with a cabin. John and Luke take position fifty meters east from the cabin. George and I stay put. We wait for half an hour. It is midafternoon. Three men exit the cabin and light cigarettes. Three shots are fired simultaneously. John and Luke take out the man in the middle and the guy on his left side. I knock the target down on the right side. We each need only one shot. We go back, get the Jeeps, and drive down to the dead targets. Three heads are blown up. We load the bodies into body bags. Two bags go into John's Jeep and one body bag into George's Jeep. George cleans some of the blood and flesh from the dirt before driving off. We unload the bodies from the bags and dump them into a sinkhole, two kilometers from the cabin. We begin to drive back toward to the ranch.

When we get to the main road, I ask George, "What do you do with the empty body bags?" "Do you use them again?"

The Bear says, "No, I'll burn them in the incinerator at the ranch. Jaime, did you think I would shoot you with my forty-five automatic, if you did not shoot the target?"

"Yes," I answer.

George says, "I would not have shot you. I would have sent you home."

"I wasn't taking any chances," I respond. "I shot the target because you showed me pictures of massacred, peasant farmers. You told me these men were responsible for killing innocent people. I could rationalize killing all three targets in my mind, so I pulled the trigger. That's it."

It is the morning of the eighth of September. I am at the Stella Maris Hotel in Mexico City. The most beautiful tall, blond, blue-eyed girl has just left me. Luke Two brought her to my hotel room last night.

He said, "She is a gift from George." She was the best gift I ever had.

Yesterday, the seventh of September, Luke and I flew from Guatemala City to Mexico City. I used the James Andrews passport. I gave the passport to Luke when we got to the hotel. Luke gave me an envelope with eight thousand dollars in it and my real passport. Luke bought me dinner. Then he brought me the girl. This morning, the eighth of September, I fly to Kennedy Airport on an Eastern Airlines flight, using my own passport.

Luke says to me, "Johnny Walker will call you at your home in New York, on September fifteenth."

It is the morning of the fifteenth of September. I meet Johnny in front of a city drugstore on East Sixteenth Street near Fifth Avenue in Manhattan. We walk a few blocks up Fifth Avenue and have breakfast in a local diner. He gives me one thousand dollars traveling money, a first class Air France plane ticket and an Alitalia plane ticket. The tickets are one way. The Air France flight is to Paris. I shall go through immigration and customs in Paris and then board a regular Alitalia flight to Rome. The reservation is in my real name and I shall use my own passport. I leave the evening of the seventeenth of September and arrive in Europe the following morning. I shall be flying alone.

The story I told my grandmother is that I have a teaching job at a private American school in Rome. I shall be home for Christmas.

It is the evening of the eighteenth of September. I am at the Hotel Quattro Fontani in Rome. Luke is in the room next to mine. He was at the hotel when I arrived. The first class Air France flight was great. The food was delicious: a prime beef with flaky crust, champagne that flowed freely, a powerful cognac and terrific stewardesses. The first class Air France flight was the second best gift I ever had. The Alitalia flight was a normal, everyday, commuter flight.

In Luke's room we go over the itinerary. He gives me the James Andrews, British passport. The passport has no entry or exit for Guatemala or Mexico. It is new again. James Andrews flew from Toronto, Canada to London, England and then to Rome. There is a visa for Angola. There is an Air Afrique plane ticket from DaVinci Airport in Rome that eventually ends up in Luanda, Angola, passing through Dakar and Abidjan. It looks like an endless flying day. I am not looking forward to this long, circuitous flight. Luke is going with me, so that makes it better. Luke tells me to leave my real passport with the person at the front desk of this hotel.

Africa

The railroad travels from Luanda to Ndalatando. This train chugs up some very steep hills. It is crowded and smelly. Luke is with me. The black Africans are speaking Portuguese. Africa is different from Mexico and Guatemala. The odor is more pungent. The hills are higher in Angola then in Guatemala and the breeze is hotter. The land runs up quickly from the coast. Some Africans are speaking another language. I would not know Bantu from Kimbundu. I am not sure if the Mbundo tribe, that lives east of Luanda, speaks Kimbundu, or the Kimbundu tribe speaks Mbundo. I am a little confused. It begins to rain.

I've been on this train before. In Guatemala I had a dream that I was on a train with Luke. George and Johnny were on the train too. I could see them in another car. White people, brown people, black people and soldiers spoke assorted languages on the train. The languages were Portuguese, Spanish, English, and strange dialects. I woke up after hearing a noise and swooshed back into my body through the top of my head. That ended the astral projection.

The plantation of Antonio Cunha is immense. It is larger than one thousand hectares or two thousand four hundred seventy acres. It is a few kilometers north of Ndaltando. The place has electricity and a generating plant. The main house has a telephone and is in the center of the plantation. Single level motel type workers housing are one hundred meters east and west from the center home. The plantation owner also communicates by short wave radio. Barns, silos and heavy tractors can be seen. The fields of rolling hills grow coffee, corn and beans. A few head of cattle, milking cows, chickens, sheep, goats, pigs and horses populate the plantation. The place is guarded by twenty-five white, Portuguese, speaking soldiers. The soldiers constantly patrol the place in Jeeps. They keep in contact by radio. From the top of the barns you can see for many kilometers in each direction.

Toward the distant north is dense wooded jungle and to the south is the district capital city of Ndaltando. Many African workers live on the plantation of Antonio Cunha.

December, 1971

It is the second of December. I have lived on the plantation for two and one half months.

I have an actual teaching job. Senor Cunha and his wife have two children at the plantation. They have an eleven year old boy Tony and a ten year old girl Lucy. The children speak excellent English. Five hours per day, five days each week I teach them basic math, writing and reading English. I tell them about life in the United States. Also, I am the children's personal bodyguard.

These kids are very smart and learn quickly. The owner's other children are in a University in the United States. This morning Senora Cunha and the two children, Tony and Lucy got onboard a single engine plane and flew to Luanda from a small airport at the west edge of Ndaltando. They are to visit the Senora's parent's home in Portugal.

Trouble is brewing and will hit the plantation shortly. I do not understand exactly what is happening. There are three alphabet soup guerilla groups: the FNLA, the MPLA and the UNITA. I assume some of these groups are communist. I know that the Portuguese colonial landowner days are numbered. The Bear wants me to gather my belongings and leave on the train to Luanda tomorrow. He says I did a fine job with the children. Senor and Senora Cunha were very pleased with me. My job is done.

Every day over the past two and one have months I practiced shooting the machine gun, sniper rifle and revolver. When I was teaching the children I kept the Smith and Wesson revolver in a knapsack. In the early evening, twice per week, I would be stationed in one of the barns with The Bear, Luke or John. We would pull a four hours shift armed with AK47s. I was never alone on the plantation. I had a private room between Luke's room and John's room. George had private quarters within the main house.

BOOM! BOOM! BOOM! Three thundering bolts rock and shock the entire plantation. The power generating plant blows up and is on fire. Artillery shells are hitting the compound. The barns and silos are burning. The Portuguese soldiers return fire. The artillery barrage suddenly stops. Swarms of attacking soldiers are moving down the hills. I see all of this from the back window of my room. I quickly get dressed. Luke, John and The Bear are at my door. They tell me to take the machine gun and the magazines of ammo. I grab the AK47 and my knapsack. It is four thirty in the morning, the third of December.

We get into position and start shooting. I have the machine gun on semi-automatic and fire one shot at a time. I see every target drop. Then I realize that there are only four shots left in this magazine. Time ceases as a hundred enemy soldiers slowly and steadily get closer.

George says, "These are well trained troops not ragtag guerillas. These soldiers are probably Cuban."

I watch George switch magazines. Luke and John are running toward the main house. George and I follow ten meters behind. A bomb blasts. Luke and John are hit. Their body parts are all over the ground. I stop for an instant and The Bear taps me on the shoulder to keep me moving. All I can think of is, "It's back to The Bardo for Johnny Walker and Luke Two."

George and I enter the large plantation house. We make our escape through a tunnel that runs from the wine cellar in the main house to a clearing near a small river, a tributary of the Cuanza River. The tunnel runs one and one half kilometers in length or ninety-three percent of one mile. The owner Antonio Cunha had the tunnel built in case of an emergency like this. George knew about the tunnel. I had no idea it existed. When we exit the tunnel we can see the plantation burning in the background.

I have the James Andrew passport and the gun in the knapsack. George told me to keep the passport with me at all times. We ditch all weapons when we reach the airfield on the outskirts of Ndalatando. This walk took over an hour.

A single engine plane is waiting with a pilot and Senor Antonio Cunha. George leads me to the plane. We get in. I do not remember what was said during the flight to Luanda.

Rome, Italy December, 1971

I am back at the Quattro Fontani Hotel in Rome. It is the ninth of December, 1971. I have been here two days. I watched the movie, *Some like It Hot,* dubbed in Italian. The guy who did the Tony Curtis voice was very good. I also saw a funny Italian movie, *Venga a Prendere Un Café Da Noi,* with Ugo Tognazzi.

George has taken me out for a couple of decent meals at a trattoria near the Treve Fountain. The Bear will shortly be getting on a plane to Paris. He asks me if I want to go with him.

The Bear says, "You are a good soldier. You performed well under fire. Are you interested in working with me again, Jaime?"

I answer. "No, I am burnt out. I want to go home. I like New York City at Christmas time. I don't want to be blown apart like Johnny and Luke."

George hands me a Pan American first class ticket in my own name. The ticket is from Rome to Kennedy Airport. He gives me twenty thousand dollars and my real passport back. I am surprised about the increase in payment.

George says, "Senor Cunha wanted you to have the extra ten thousand dollars."

I fly from Rome to New York City on December 10, 1971. The Air France first class flight was much better than the Pan American flight.

Back to Present July, 1980

My mind returns to the present. The year is nineteen hundred eighty. The time is 2:30 AM and the date is the fifth of July. I am almost finished writing this story. I was a willing participant in the Guatemalan and African affairs that affected me the rest of my life. I am not able to sleep more than three hours in a night. Two years ago I had a dream about Africa. I woke up in a cold sweat. I was terrified. I have dreams of being in battles and getting killed. Sometimes bullets go into me. Sometimes knifes stick into me. Sometimes I get blown up. Then after I die, I get up and the battle starts again. It never ends. I can count the friends I have on one hand. I cannot hold a job for more than a few months. I can only read and study in small bits and pieces. It is difficult for me to learn new courses at a university. I have to take Valium before getting on an airplane. Other than that I'm fine.

I put down my pen and close my notebook. I turn the radio on low to listen to an American music pop station. Steely Dan sings, "You go back Jack do it again."

Today after many years, I saw The Funny Bear again. The phone is ringing. Who could this possibly be at this hour of the night? I pick up the telephone.

It is The Bear, he says, *"Que hubo, Jaime!"*

Book III: GERM SPREADERS ON A TRAIN

New York City, February, 1998

It is February 1, 1998. The advertisement in the help wanted section of the New York Sunday newspaper states: "Wanted Mature Adult for General Bookkeeping and Accounting; MS Word and Excel required; Knowledge of Statistics is a plus. Fax Resume to L&J Incorporated; telephone 212 etc."

I fax my resume. I am in dire need of a job. I had worked for a small family billing business in Newark, New Jersey. The old couple that employed me sold the business, retired and moved to Florida. For three years I did billing, accounting, general bookkeeping and taxes for the company. It had been a pleasant, stress free job. The past two months I missed going to work and even missed commuting on the train.

Today I have the job interview. It is Tuesday the tenth of February. I jump on the number six local subway train at Lexington Avenue and Seventy-Seventh Street. I get off at the Brooklyn Bridge station and walk around City Hall. I continue to walk down Chambers Street to Broadway. Then I go up Broadway passing by Federal Plaza. As I continue walking, I realize that I should have gotten off the subway at Canal Street. Finally I find the building and go inside. A security guard points me toward the elevator. On the seventh floor at exactly 9:45 AM, I knock on the door of L&J Incorporated.

Two large young men open the door and greet me. The first young fellow has light brown skin and the second young man has fair skin. They say in unison, "Good Morning."

The brown man says, "My name is Danny Johnson."

"My name is Louis Rodriguez," says his partner. "Your resume shows that you live on the Upper East Side, near York Avenue?"

"Yes," I answer.

Danny says, "You're in good shape for," he stopped.

I complete his sentence, "an old guy."

"How old are you?" asks Louis.

"Forty nine," I answer

"Well," says Danny, "you are exactly what we are looking for. Why did you leave your last job?"

"The owners sold the company and retired. Here is the name, address and phone number of my prior employers." I hand Danny the references.

Louis questions, "You have an advanced degree in statistics. How come you work as an accountant?"

"No one would hire me as a statistician. So I switched to accounting and was able to get a job as a bookkeeper."

Then I ask, "What does the L and J stand for in L&J Incorporated?"

"For the gospels, Luke and John in the Bible," says Danny. I think, "Jeez."

Danny and Louis hire me immediately. At 10:15 AM, Tuesday the tenth of February, 1998, I go to work for L&J Incorporated.

January, 2001

It is now January, 2001. I have been working with L&J Inc. for three years. This is what I know.

Although Louis and Danny were brought up in Manhattan they didn't know one another. They met at graduate school in Massachusetts. They became friends and shared an apartment in Cambridge a few blocks from the Charles River and the MIT dome. Upon graduation in May, 1996, they opened up L&J Incorporated. The money for the business came from the sale of a software program they designed and patented. L&J Incorporated is a Biotechnology Consulting Firm.

In graduate school, Louis and Danny developed a software program. The program is used for genetic engineering, coding and replication of DNA. By implementing a Monte Carlo simulation, the software program dices and splices the proper combination of messenger RNA molecules and builds proteins. This software is licensed to a major company in Silicon Valley, California. The California Company manufactures and sells the program to biotech firms all over the world. Louis and Danny get a small percentage from each sale.

Danny and Louis earn more money as consultants. They have consulting contracts with thirteen clients. Two companies are based in Boston. Two companies are in Northern New Jersey, three in California, one in Nevada, one in Memphis and one pharmaceutical company in New York City. They have a contract with the United States Government. They have two foreign clients located in London and Paris. L&J Incorporated consult with companies that manufacture new medicines and vaccines, investigate the causation of genetically inherited diseases, clone organisms and do stem cell research. One company they consult with is developing a thinking computer chip based on organic molecules and neuronal cells. The program can also be applied for the development of bacterium and viruses used for germ warfare.

Louis Rodriquez was born in New York City on the seventeenth of November, 1973. He lives on East Eighty-Third Street. He is six feet tall, one hundred seventy pounds. He is light complexioned, good-looking and extremely intelligent.

Louis went through the New York City Public School System. He graduated City University with a double major in biochemistry and computer science. He received a Master's Degree in Software Engineering from MIT in 1996. His mother was half Irish and half Puerto Rican. She was a grade school teacher, born in Manhattan.   She died suddenly of a heart attack at home on the fourth of July 1996. Louis never knew his father. His mother told him that his father died a few months before he was born. She said his dad was killed in Vietnam.

Danny Johnson was born in Jersey City, New Jersey the twenty-eighth of November, 1973. Danny lives on West Seventy-Eighth Street. He is six feet two inches tall, two hundred ten pounds. He has light brown skin. Danny is also highly intelligent, very handsome and powerfully built.

Danny attended Catholic Schools. He graduated from Manhattanville College with degrees in biology and computer science. Danny received his Master's Degree in Software

Engineering from MIT in 1996. Danny's mother was a gynecologist, born in Newark, New Jersey. She was of African American and Italian decent. She was a tall, slender woman. The cleaning crew found her dead at her office desk, late on a Thursday evening, the nineteenth of September 1996. The autopsy showed a brain aneurysm. Danny told me that his father died of a colon cancer when he was eighteen months old. Danny said he did not remember his father at all. Danny is very proud of the accomplishments of his mother.

I find that the personal interests of these two young guys are the same. Danny and Louis both listen to classic rock music. They play songs from the sixties. They listen to an oldies station on WCBS 101.1 FM and listen to a rock station at 104.3 FM.

"You can't always get what you want." Danny Johnson sings that line, every now and then. Then he sings, "I know it's only rock and roll." Danny is a big Rolling Stones fan.

Louis sings, "I'm doing time on cloud nine." Sometimes he sings, "You need schooling, I ain't fooling." I never heard a young guy sing a song by the Temptations and then another song by Led Zepplen. They remind me of guys from the sixties because their taste in music ends in the year, 1971.

I think, "Where are the hip hop, rap and salsa?"

Every Wednesday evening Danny and Louis meet at a karate club near Amsterdam Avenue and Seventy-Second Street. Sometimes they run together in a Central Park race. Occasionally I'll join them for a race in the park. Of course they always wait for me at the finish line.

During the three years I have been with L&J Incorporated hardly anyone has ever entered the office suite. Danny and Louis work with minimal distractions. It is a business office like any other with computers, telephones, copiers, and fax machines. Each one of us has a private room. My office room is in the front between Danny's office and Louis's office. Each room is the same size. There are also a meeting room, bathroom and shower in the large office suite. There is a good view of lower Broadway from the meeting room.

Danny and Louis are extremely security conscious. They
send encrypted email and have firewalls set on the network
system server. Hackers have been unable to crash into their
system. L&J Incorporated has a business website. I monitor
the website logs. I try to track where virus attacks come from.
Most of the attacks come from anonymous web addresses.
These anonymous addresses are listed on a Russian website.

Danny and Louis travel by airplane to California, Nevada,
Tennessee, France and Great Britain. They take the Amtrak
train to Boston and Washington, D.C. I make all travel
arrangements for them. I am responsible for local consulting
correspondence in New York City and New Jersey.

The guys date women from all over the world. I have met a
few of their girlfriends at small private parties given at Danny's
apartment. These young women are extremely good looking.

The company L&J Incorporated has gross receipts of six
hundred eighty thousand dollars before taxes for the year ended
December 31, 2000. Seventy five percent of the receipts come
from consulting fees. The other quarter of revenue is from
their percentage of software sales. Louis and Danny are doing
rather well.

It is another cold January day. As usual I travel on the
subway train to and from work. The commuters on these
transit trains have some nasty colds. They wheeze and sneeze.
They carry tissues and cough drops. I try to avoid them. When
I'm on a train, if possible, I move my seat to get away from the
germ spreaders. I am paranoid about catching a cold. I make
sure I take plenty of vitamin C before getting on any train.

Business Trip

Today is my first long distance business trip for L&J
Incorporated. It is Tuesday, the twenty-third of January, 2001.
I board the Lake Shore Limited to Chicago at New York Penn
Station. I have a small first class room. I shall transfer trains
at Union Station in Chicago for the train westward. I always
wanted to take a train to Chicago, riding through western,
upstate New York to the Great Lakes. I remember watching
Cary Grant in *North by Northwest* traveling on the Twentieth

Century Limited from New York Grand Central Station to Chicago. Now I am traveling on a train to the Windy City.

There are no pretty actresses on this train. There are only *Twilight Zone People*. I speak with them in the dining car. The *Twilight Zone People* are all afraid to fly. Some have been on hijacked airplanes. They have lots of interesting stories. I listen to them.

In Buffalo, I get off the train and stand outside the station. I think of a movie, where a famous actor, I think Gene Hackman, plays a policeman, traveling on a train through Western Canada. It is really cold in Buffalo, New York; probably just as cold as Western Canada.

On Wednesday, the twenty-fourth of January, I arrive in Chicago. Before I change trains for the western part of the trip, I go directly to the Amtrak counter and rearrange my travel itinerary. There is a closed circuit camera above the ticket booth. It takes pictures of passengers purchasing tickets. The original train tickets are for Las Vegas with a return trip to New York City on Monday, the twenty-ninth of January. I pay an extra fee and change my return ticket to depart from Union Station in Los Angeles, California on Sunday, the fourth of February, 2001. Therefore I shall be in Las Vegas for Super Bowl weekend. Then I shall visit Los Angeles, California.

I board the train heading west out of Chicago, Illinois at 4:15 PM Central Time. This train has an upstairs and downstairs. It has a viewing car too. The train travels through Illinois, crosses the Mississippi River into Iowa then goes through Missouri, Kansas and a piece of Colorado. The train chugs into the tunnel at the Santa Fe Pass through the Rocky Mountains to New Mexico. There is some light snow flurry activity in the mountains. It is a dreary day. Finally the train comes down from Flagstaff, Arizona to the desert. I and six other passengers get off the train in the middle of the night in Needles, California. The train then continues to its final destination in Los Angeles.

We seven passengers take a shuttle van from Needles to Las Vegas, Nevada. Elvis is with us. When we were on the train, he sang a few songs for some of the girls. Of course he is just an Elvis impersonator but his presence makes the trip a little more bizarre.

The van takes us to McCarran Airport in Las Vegas. I grab a taxi from the airport to the Luxor Hotel. The taxi driver gives me a card for a nightclub with lap dancers. Everybody is on the hustle in Vegas. Las Vegas is a lot like New York City.

I am inside my hotel room. It is 4:00 AM Pacific Time, Friday, the twenty-sixth of January. The trip took two and one half days.

On Saturday, the twenty-seventh of January I have to do my job. I take a taxi to North Las Vegas. I punch in a code to open the gate into a private community. The gate opens and the cab driver takes me to the directed address. I ring the doorbell at precisely noon. An elderly man answers the door. I hand him one computer floppy diskette. Then I get back into the taxi and return to my hotel.

I have some relatives in Vegas. Saturday evening, I go with them to a famous restaurant inside the Venice Hotel. I eat some pasta and Caesar salad. I drink a little red wine and have a cup of espresso for desert. The food is good and less expensive than New York. After returning to the hotel and casino, I play some video poker and lose twenty dollars. An old song by Steely Dan comes into my thoughts, "Now you find yourself in Vegas." During the evening, a blond, blue eyed, very pretty, cocktail waitress in her mid-thirties stops to look at me. She reminds me of the sister of a girl I once knew many years ago. I say nothing to her and go to listen to the Blue Man Group bang away on the drums. The Blue Man Group does shows in New York City too. However, I never went to see them in Manhattan.

Sunday afternoon, I watch the Super Bowl in the large, hotel theater with my cousins and their friends. There are lots of hot dogs, beer, people and fun. The football game is between the Giants and the Ravens. I win $100 betting on the over. The final score is Ravens 34 and Giants 7.

Monday morning, the twenty-ninth of January, I take the local Greyhound Bus from downtown Las Vegas to Los Angeles. I know I am being followed. The guy watching me gets off the bus in Barstow. He made it clear to me I was being monitored. He was either a Las Vegas policeman or a local FBI guy. I wasn't sure which.

The bus ride to Los Angeles takes more than seven hours. I should have taken the express bus.

From the LA bus station, I grab a taxi to Torrance, another forty- five minutes in traffic.

My Uncle Bill picks me up at the Tally Ho apartment complex in Torrance, California. He brings me out to dinner and then to his home in Rolling Hills. Rolling Hills is a guarded hilltop community. No one gets in without the consent of the guards.

I have three deliveries to make in California. My uncle gives me his car, an Audi, very fast. On Tuesday, I deliver one diskette to a physician in Newport Beach. On Wednesday, I make two diskette deliveries, one to a clinic in Downey and another to a residence in Long Beach. That is it. My work for L&J Incorporated is done.

Now I visit some old friends. Thursday evening, we have dinner at an Italian restaurant at the Fashion Mall in Newport Beach. On Friday, I have dinner with some other friends at their home in Seal Beach. It is a nice time.

On Sunday, the fourth of February, I board the train at Union Station, Los Angeles. There is a government agent behind me, making sure I get on the train. I think he is probably from the east coast and not California because he is wearing a suit. The temperature is eighty-seven degrees Fahrenheit. It is a very hot day for early February in Los Angeles.

There are some problems on the return trip. The porter tells me, a freight train derailed outside of Winslow, Arizona. A song by the Eagles plays through my mind, "I'm standing on a corner in Winslow, Arizona."

The train cannot go around the derailment. The other passengers and I have to take buses to Albuquerque, New Mexico, a four hundred miles ride through Flagstaff, Arizona, on Interstate-40. I know the route well because I have driven this highway a half dozen times in my life. This is an eight hours bus ride and I get to see some high desert scenery.

In Albuquerque we get on the train that was heading west. Now this train goes east. The passengers on the western bound train do the same thing in reverse. When their bus arrives in Winslow, Arizona they board the original train I was on and head west. Because of the long delay, I miss my connecting train when I arrive in Chicago. Therefore, I have to spend one night at the Days Inn Hotel in Chicago before changing trains for New York City the next evening.

When I arrive at New York Penn Station on Thursday, the eighth of February, I quickly leave the train. The same government agent who had checked the train in Los Angeles peers at me exiting the train in New York. The watchers are watching me.

Return to Work

On Monday, the twelfth of February, I return to work. Louis and Danny ask if the deliveries went smoothly.

I answer, "Yes, but I was followed."

Louis says, "Who followed you?"

I answer, "The government. I was checked throughout the trip. Amtrak is regulated by the government, therefore the government can make inquiries about the arrival and departure of everyone that goes on the train. Any government security agency can check hotels, bus lines, whatever. They just check the credit cards and schedules. There are cameras in the train station, bus station and all over the place in the hotels in Las Vegas. There is Amtrak security on the train. It is really easy to monitor anyone. The government can also get records of all cell phone calls and bank card withdrawals with the exact time and place."

Danny states, "You were probably followed because of our government contracts."

I say, "Yes, I assumed that was the reason." I fail to mention to them that I may be followed for numerous motives.

Danny adds, "Where you ever watched by anyone else since you've been working for us?"

"Yes," I answer. "I went to a movie on East Eighty-Sixth Street. It was a nine o'clock show on a Saturday night, last

September. The theater was crowded and I took a seat toward the front. A young couple watched me. The male was early thirties, white, well built, six feet tall and clean clothes. The female was late twenties, blond, nice looking, athletic, five ten and wearing dark pants. They sat three rows behind me. I felt them watching me. Fifteen minutes into the movie, I got up and went to the bathroom. I was in the bathroom one minute. When I opened the door to leave, that guy was coming in. I immediately left the theatre."

"What do you think they wanted?" Louis questions.

"I have no idea."

Danny says. "Maybe the guy had to go to the bathroom."

"No," I answer. "The girl was at the candy counter when I left the theater. She saw me leave. When I got onto the street, it was crowded. I quickly walked down Eighty-Sixth Street, than I ducked into the Barnes and Noble bookstore. I saw the guy and girl pass by the bookstore window shortly thereafter."

"Then what did you do?" asks Louis.

"I left the bookstore, walked in the opposite direction to Lexington Avenue, went down into the subway and took the number six train to Seventy-Seventh Street. Then I got off the train and went home."

"What was the movie?" asks Danny.

"It was a movie about cloning, starring Arnold. It was absolutely awful. I would have walked out on it anyway." I did not tell Danny and Louis, that I stopped going to movies on Saturday nights. Now I go to the movies afternoons only.

"How come you never told us about these two people?" says Louis.

"It probably had nothing to do with L&J Incorporated. In New York City, people watch other people all the time. There can be lots of reasons they were watching me. I figure they may have had me confused with someone else. Or because they saw I was alone, they may have wanted to hold me up, take my wallet, whatever. So, I got away from this young couple as quickly as possible."

Louis says, "It may have had something to do with our company. Danny and I started getting followed in June, 2000.

We have government contracts so we notified the Federal Bureau of Investigation in the city. The government offered us protection from corporate spies. They wanted to monitor our Internet connection. We refused the offer because we are capable of protecting our computer system. After analyzing reasons for this new surveillance we realized it was the government following us."

Danny then says, "We did not tell you about the government watching us because we did not want you to get upset and quit the job. We know you like privacy and don't want any unnecessary problems."

"Don't worry about it," I say. "This job adds some excitement to my peaceful, boring, mundane life. You both have always been honest with me. You told me the disks contain a computer worm that destroys the network systems of your Nevada and California companies."

Danny responds, "Those disks are meant to crash L&J's computer program in case one of those companies begins to use the program for biological weapons development."

I think, "Germ spreading."

"How was the trip?" asks Louis.

"On the return trip, a freight train derailed in Arizona. We had to get on buses all the way to New Mexico. The kid behind me on the bus had a terrible cold and coughed for three hundred miles."

"A germ spreader," says Louis.

"Yes, I answer." "I caught a mild cold for two days. The first cold I had in seven years."

September 11, 2001

I have a small home on the New Jersey shore. After making some extra money, I had a contractor build the house in October, 1982.

In 1995, I purchased a brand new Toyota Corolla. I don't drive the car much, so after six years the Toyota is in very good condition. I never take the car to New York City. I just keep the car at the house in New Jersey.

On Tuesday, the eleventh of September, I am at the Jersey shore purchasing food in a Shop Right Store. I get into my car and turn on the radio. The disc jockey says, "A plane flew into the World Trade Center. What the hell is going on? How could someone fly a plane into that building?" Then the DJ says, "This must be a terrorist attack that the government will try to cover up." Then a second plane hits. The disc jockey says, "This is definitely a terrorist attack and the government can't cover it up."

When I get home, I watch the horror on television. It is like seeing a movie, not real. I write in my logbook, Tuesday, September 11, 2001, WTC goes down.

I stay in New Jersey until Friday morning and then take a train back to New York City. As the train approaches New York from the Jersey side, I see smoldering smoke where the World Trade Center once stood.

I had witnessed the construction of the World Trade Center from about 1967 through 1973. I recently had dinner there at one of the restaurants in the mall. It is hard for me to believe that the entire complex is destroyed.

During the past six months the L&J company website has been bombarded with viruses. The viruses do not get through because of a firewall set up on a server in Connecticut. This past week before the eleventh of September, there was a hit every second on the website. There were a total of one million hits for the week. The viruses are named red and blue. I am not sure why they are called that. I now realize there is a new kind of germ warfare out in cyberspace. The attackers will spread enough viruses to electronically break down communication links. These attackers are very smart and very organized. They are the new germ spreaders.

Danny and Louis return from London on Sunday, the sixteenth of September. They come directly to my apartment. We have had no contact since their departure for Europe the previous week. They say they saw the World Trade Center attack on television.

Louis speaks first, "People were jumping from the buildings."

"They did not show the jumpers very much on television here," I answer.

Danny asks me. "How do you think something like that could happen?"

I say, "The government can track all planes by the Norad system. Our fighter pilots probably would not shoot down the commercial airliners that crashed into the World Trade Center buildings or the Pentagon building. They may have shot down the plane in Pennsylvania."

Danny says, "Louis and I are going to allow the worm to destroy our programs in the pharmaceutical companies in Paris and London."

"Why," I ask?

"Because the company in London has an affiliation with Iraq and the Paris company has connections with Iran," he answers.

Then Louis says, "Do you understand how the worm procedure is initiated."

"Yes, you have a specific date and time code. If you don't return to those companies within a certain period of time to update the code then the sequence for destruction will start."

Danny says, "We won't be returning to London and Paris. They can fix the problems the computer virus will cause in a few weeks. They can find other consultants."

I say, "When the worm destroys their network they may want you two guys to fix the problem."

"L&J Incorporated will be unavailable when that happens," speaks Louis.

I say, "Why?"

Danny says, "Louis and I are going to enlist in the army tomorrow. With your help we shall keep part of the business going for the next year."

I say, "Are you both sure you want to do join the army?"

"Yes," they answer in unison."

I know that Louis and Danny have made up their minds and I will be unable to change their decision. But I try anyway.

I say, "You both can be anything you want. You can go back to school and become doctors, college professors, anything. You can become rich from this business. L&J Incorporated has gross receipts of $809,000 for this year and the year is not over."

They smile at me and leave.

Over the next few weeks we are all very busy reorganizing L&J Incorporated. Louis flies to Nevada and California with some computer disks. These disks will remove the worms I had delivered to those companies the past February. Louis gives notice to the western companies that L&J Incorporated will not be doing any more consulting. Louis then recommends another consulting firm. After completion of business in California, he takes a flight from LAX to Memphis. It takes Louis two days to complete work at the Memphis genetics research firm. When he gets back to New York, he tells me that I will have to visit Tennessee in the future.

Danny takes care of business at the two companies in New Jersey and the other company in Manhattan. These three companies are pharmaceutical firms. They will not need any future consulting because their contracts expire with L&J Incorporated this coming December. Danny tells me that I am capable of handling any software problems with these local companies over the next few months. I can contact him or Louis if I have any questions.

Next, Danny flies to Boston. After three days working with the two companies there, he jumps on an American Airlines flight at Logan Airport and goes to Washington D.C. The government contract is with the Department of Defense located in Arlington, Virginia. If the government needs any help with the computer program they can consult with either of the Boston firms. The government can also find Danny and Louis at any time. They are entering the army shortly.

L&J Incorporated will close the office on Broadway when the lease runs out in May, 2002. I am going to give up my apartment on the East Side and move into Louis's apartment on East Eighty Third Street. Louis owns a large three bedroom apartment with an extra maid's bedroom. Louis has set up an office in the maid's room. I will take the smallest bedroom. Louis will keep his bedroom and the other bedroom will be setup for Danny.

Danny owns a very large two bedroom West Side condominium. He tells me to lease the fully furnished apartment after he and Louis leave for the army. My job is to keep L&J Incorporated in business for a little while longer. It should not be difficult. I shall collect the royalties on program sales from the Silicon Valley Company and answer all correspondence. Danny and Louis tell me that I have a clear understanding of the functionality of the computer program. I can do consulting work. I shall consult with the two companies in Boston and the company in Memphis.

My understanding of the computer program starts with the definition of a Monte Carlo simulation. "A Monte Carlo Simulation is a spreadsheet simulation, which randomly generates values for uncertain variables over and over to stimulate a model."

These simulations are mostly used in risk analysis. Danny and Louis have a few textbooks on this subject. However when there is something I don't understand, I go to the Internet and do a web search. I type in "Monte Carlo Simulation" and I get websites with definitions, explanations and software all pertaining to a Monte Carlo Simulation.

What the L&J Incorporated software program does is this. It joins the proper combinations of messenger RNA molecules. These messenger RNA molecules are composed of several hundreds or thousands of unpaired straight strands. They contain codons that are exactly complementary to the code words of the genes. There are about twenty-five thousand genes in human DNA. It is the proteins made from the genes that will cure illness. Danny and Louis's program builds protein models. The program takes the amino acids, adenine, guanine, cytosine and thymine, (uracil in RNA), places them into the Monte Carlo Simulation and codes a gene sequence.

It is a good thing that over the past few years I have read many articles about genetics in scientific and medical journals. Prior to this job the last time I studied genetics was just after Gregory Mendel grew his first flowers. Anyway, I could always contact Louis or Danny if I have problems writing computer code.

On Monday, the fifth of November, 2001 Danny and Louis leave for Fort Benning, Georgia. It is one day after the marathon in the city. The boys passed their preliminary physical exams a few weeks earlier in Manhattan. The exam consisted of chin-ups, pushups, sit-ups, a one-mile run and some agility drills. They both ran a mile under six minutes. They easily completed twenty chin-ups, one hundred pushups and one hundred sit-ups in a few minutes. Danny and Louis are only a few weeks away from their twenty-eighth birthdays. I assume the age limit for Officer's Candidate School is twenty-eight years old. Danny and Louis meet the age qualifying limit. I read on the army website that the age requirement for special candidates can be waved up to thirty-four years old. These guys are certainly special candidates for officer training. I am sure they scored extremely high on the intelligence tests.

After the attack on the World Trade Center many young men and women enlist in the armed forces. Some of the new recruits are older enlistees such as Danny and Louis. However most are very young only 18 and 19 years old.

I remember when I was in Chicago nine months earlier. I saw young men and women sailors stationed at the Naval Base at Lake Michigan. They looked like children. It felt funny to me that these young kids were in the Navy to protect me. I felt that I should be protecting them. Shortly, these sailors will be going into a real war. I consider all the young soldiers and sailors true believers. They have a calling to protect people.

   The firemen and policemen in New York City are also true
believers. They give up their lives to help save innocent people
every day. Then there are the health care workers, doctors and
nurses. Their job is to heal the sick and injured. They dedicate
their lives to help others. They are all heroes to me. I wish
that I were like them but I am not. I am not a true believer of
anything.

   Danny and Louis spend nine weeks in Basic Combat Training
at Fort Benning, Georgia. After completion of their basic army
course they have a few days leave. Next they enter Officers
Training School also at Fort Benning. It is fourteen weeks of
very difficult training.

   On Saturday, the twentieth of April, 2002, Danny and Louis
graduate from Officer's Candidate School as second
lieutenants. I am unable to attend their graduation ceremony. I
have to go over data documentation procedures that involve the
Boston companies. They tell me in an email, "It is more
important for me to do the work involving the Boston
companies then to attend their graduation ceremonies."

   After graduating OCS, the boys do not return to New York
for leave. They go directly to Fort Bragg, North Carolina for a
thirty days course in Special Forces training with the Eighty
Second Airborne. I figure they will be jumping from airplanes.

   Danny and Louis send me copies of their military graduation
pictures. I place Danny's picture next to a picture of his
mother on his bedroom bureau. I do the same with Louis's
picture. Louis has a small snapshot of his mother and father.
In this photograph his parents are dressed in bell-bottomed blue
jeans. They are very young. Louis has the same light
complexion as his mother. I also have a picture of Danny and
Louis together. They look very similar in the army dress
uniforms. Danny's skin color is shaded darker but he
definitely resembles Louis.

   In May, 2002 I close the L&J Incorporated office on lower
Broadway. The lease has expired. I leave the city to spend the
summer months on the Jersey shore. I travel back into New
York City twice a week to collect mail and take care of
business. Rather than drive the car, I take the North Jersey

Coast Line Train. Most of my correspondence with Danny and Louis is done by email. They do not write letters or talk on the telephone. I have a personal aversion to the telephone. You never know who is listening to your private conversation. I do carry a cell phone. In case of an emergency I can call 911 or I can use it as a weapon.

Danny and Louis left some large files with me before they went into the army. I added data and documentation to those files.

Danny said, "Just keep the files safe."

I brought the files to my house in New Jersey.

On Saturday, the second of June, 2002, Danny and Louis fly to San Francisco, California. They are attending the Army Language School in Monterrey, California. They will be stationed there for almost six months. They have intensive language training. Danny will learn Arabic and Louis will study Dari. Danny and Louis are already fluent in Spanish and French. They send me an email saying, "We shall enjoy learning these different alphabets and languages."

On Friday, the thirtieth of August, Danny emails me instructions. He and Louis want me to go to Boston and Memphis to complete some business with the biotechnology firms in those cities. The instructions tell me I will have to work in Boston. They leased a furnished apartment for me. It is a four months lease that begins on Wednesday, the fourth of September and ends on Tuesday, the thirty-first of December.

September, 2002

On Tuesday, the third of September, I drive from the Jersey Shore to Wakefield, Massachusetts. It is the day after Labor Day. I take the Garden State Parkway from Exit 98 all the way to the last rest stop in New Jersey. After my fifteen minutes break, the ride continues onto Interstate Highway 287 in New York State. I drive over the Tappan Zee Bridge into Westchester County. There are "Men at Work" signs. They have been repairing this highway for twenty years. Perhaps they are just about done. I pass an exit for Westchester Avenue and Purchase, New York. I believe that exit goes to Manhattanville College where Danny attended school.

The car drives through Connecticut on Interstate 95. The ride is not going badly. The tollbooths had been taken down years ago. This used to be a horrible ride. You had to stop and pay a toll every few miles. The truck drivers would slam into the tollbooths at night. They would get injured or killed. Finally the tolls were taken down and the state of Connecticut put safety before greed.

New Jersey is a greedy state too. There are tolls every few miles on the Garden State Parkway but there are no large trucks allowed on the road north of Long Branch. Therefore the ride in New Jersey is safer on the parkway. If I had chosen to take the New Jersey Turnpike, I would have had to deal with the giant trucks and still pay tolls when exiting the road.

However, the state that takes the cake for greed is New York State. Wherever there is a bridge or a tunnel in the State of New York you pay a toll fee.

I continue my ride through Bridgeport, Connecticut. A few miles further there is an exit for Trumbull. The company that provides the computer server for L&J Incorporated is located in Trumbull.

At the Madison exit, I pull off the road to find a McDonald's. This is the farthest point I had ever previously driven into New England. I knew a girl from this area long ago. It was her sister I saw in Las Vegas in January, 2001. I try not to think of the past. It is best to have my memories blurred. A Steely Dan song plays inside my head, "You'll be on your knees tomorrow."

I think, "Yeah, right." The road is new to me from this point onward.

There is light highway traffic through the rest of Connecticut. Traffic gets heavier as I approach Cranston and Providence, Rhode Island. I stay on Highway 95. More cars enter the highway in Massachusetts. I circumvent the city of Boston and arrive at my final destination, the Best Western Hotel in Wakefield, Massachusetts. This trip took over seven hours and was two hundred eighty-five miles.

One of the biotech firms is named WFD Genetic Engineering, located in Wakefield, a northern suburb of Boston. When I received the email from Danny a few days ago I immediately called the WFD office. I set a meeting with a Mr. Scott for 9:00 AM Wednesday, the forth of September, 2002.

At 8:40 AM, Wednesday, I drive one mile into the WFD office complex. It is a medium size, gray, three stories building with ample parking spaces in the back. After parking my Toyota, I walk about thirty yards and enter the rear of the building. I report to the security office and show the security guard my driver's license for identification. He confirms my appointment with Mr. Scott. Then the guard places a visitor's badge on my jacket and directs me to the elevator. Mr. Scott's office is on the third floor. I knock on the door and a male voice with a Mid-Western accent says, "Come in." Mr. Scott is a young man. He is strongly built, six feet in height, fair complexion. He is not wearing a suit. He is a graduate school buddy of Danny and Louis. He is the owner and president of the genetic engineering firm. He has a picture of himself, his wife and two young sons on his office desk next to his computer. They are a good-looking American family. There is no secretary in his office.

He tells me to call him, "Scotty."

All I can think of is, "Beam me up."

Scotty explains what Danny and Louis want me to do. I am to work on an offline computer in the small office adjoining his. He tells me to make my own schedule concerning when I want to work.

I say, "I can work here Monday and Tuesday from 8:30 AM to 4:00 PM, if that's Ok with you?"

Scotty says, "Fine, but you have to go down to the security office and have your picture taken. The security guard will make a WFD Identification for you, than you can come into the building without any hassles." He adds, "Where are you staying?"

"L&J Incorporated leased an apartment for me in Woburn. I am going there now," I answer.

Scotty says, "Did you stay there last night?"

"No, I stayed at the Best Western Hotel up the road."

"See you Monday," says Scotty.

"Ok, bye."

I leave and walk down the stairs to the security office. The guard takes a photographic of me. I return my visitor's pass. I wait a few moments and he hands me a new personal identification badge with my photo affixed.

The guard says, "Welcome to WFD."

I exit the building and get into my car. Now, I have to find my apartment. Woburn is two towns over, about five miles away. I have to key my travel position on the map. The main highway is Highway 128. That is Interstate 95. The other roads are labyrinthine. It will take me a couple of weeks to learn the back roads.

It is almost a half hour before I find the apartment complex. If I knew where I was going, the ride would have taken ten minutes. I find the apartment manager's office. It is a big office with four large desks, with four women, one at each desk. I ask the girl at the front desk for the manager. She points toward the woman at the largest desk in the back of the room. The three women at the front desks are young, in their late twenties. The manager is about ten years older.

I say, "I represent L&J Incorporated and I am here for the apartment."

She pulls out the lease and I sign it. The lease is made out to L&J Incorporated. I am controller of the company and have power of attorney to sign for all financial activities. The rent is thirteen hundred dollars per month which includes: heat, electricity and cable television with HBO. I write out a company check for twenty-six hundred dollars. The payment is for the first month's rent and a month's security deposit. I will only have to pay October and November rent. December is covered with the security deposit. This seems to be a very good deal.

She says, "How are Danny and Louis doing?"

I answer, "They are doing fine."

"Do they like being in army?"

"Yes, I think they do."

Then she says, "I got an email from them last week and arranged the apartment for you." She hands me the keys and calls the superintendent.

I follow him through the apartment complex. The complex includes: a swimming pool, gym, tennis courts and basketball courts. A parking lot is in front of each of the four apartment buildings. Every building has three sections or entrances. All buildings have a ground, middle and upper floor. Each floor has two apartments.

So, I think, "Four buildings, times three sections, times three floors, times two apartments, equals seventy-two individual apartments. The set up reminds me of the apartment complexes I saw in California, February of 2001.

My apartment is a ground floor apartment. There is a front door entrance and an entrance from the street side. Therefore, I can pull my car around to the back door of the apartment and easily unload it.

The living room is very large but sparsely furnished with one couch and two large chairs. There is a fair sized television set. A small dining area with a table and four chairs is set between the living room and kitchen. The kitchen has a dishwasher, four burner electric stove, large oven and microwave oven. Dishes, cups, saucers and utensils are supplied for four people. There is a frying pan and spatula, a couple of pots and a soup ladle. The bedroom is large with a queen size bed, dresser and lamp. There also is an alarm clock radio. The bathroom has a normal bath and shower. This apartment is four times the size of my old apartment on East Seventy-Eighth Street. It is half the size of Louis's East Eighty-Third Street apartment.

In the hallway between my apartment and the next one is a room with a washing machine and dryer. That specific washer is for the six apartments in this section.

The superintendent asks, "Is the apartment OK?"

"It is fine," I answer.

I offer him a ten-dollar tip, but he does not take it. This place is not like New York City.

I move my car to the back street behind the apartment. I have some stuff to unload. The stuff includes: a combined CD, tape and radio set, a laptop computer and L&J Incorporated files. There is one good suit, four pairs of pants, seven shirts and twelve pairs of socks, a dozen undergarments, six tee shirts, gym shorts and a sweat suit. I brought one extra pair of black dress shoes and two pairs of sneakers. A few towels, a set of sheets and a couple of blankets are the final items I bring into the apartment. I shall need to go shopping to purchase a few more things.

I return to the manager's office and ask the girl at the front desk. "Where are a department store and the Woburn train station?"

She says, "There is a Target store and the train station is up the road from the store. You just head north on Highway 128 and get off at the next exit. Then make a left and another left and you will see the Woburn Mall. After the mall, make a quick right turn onto Commerce Way. Go straight for a mile and you will see the Target Store. You can't miss it. If you continue on Commerce Way for another couple of miles, you will see a sign for the Woburn Train Station. Make a left at the sign and you will be there. Oh, there is also a post office if you bear left at Exit 36 on Washington Street."

"Is that the exit I take from Highway 128, Exit 36 Washington Street?"

"Yes," she answers.

When I get into my car, I check my map. Her directions look good. There are back roads to Commerce Way through Mishawum Road. I will have to figure those roads out later.

When I get to the Target store and leave my car, I check around. I am looking for unmarked white vans. I don't see any. During the summer in New Jersey, I would occasionally see unmarked white vans pass my house. A van would pass in the middle of the night or the middle of the day. I don't see any of them now. Most of the white vans in New York City are usually for small business. They have the company name on the sides of the van. Unmarked white vans make me nervous.

In the Target store, I purchase an extra set of sheets, towels, shower curtain and a can opener.

Next I drive a couple miles north on Commerce Way and turn left at the train station sign onto Atlantic Avenue. The Woburn Station is named the Anderson-Woburn Station. It is a good size transportation center. The center has both long and short-term parking lots. I park in the commuter lot, check the parking space number and pay a buck at a machine. There is a bus leaving for Logan Airport outside the terminal.

Inside the train terminal there is a large board that lists departing flights from Logan Airport. Two customer service windows are open. These windows are where you pay for the Logan Bus shuttle, commuter train tickets, Amtrak train tickets and long-term parking. I notice that the long-term parking rates are four dollars per day. I feel that rate is expensive. I pick up a commuter train schedule for the Massachusetts Bay Transit Authority. This commuter line is the Lowell line. Lowell is a town north of here. A round trip ticket to Boston is six dollars and fifty cents. I walk over to the Dunkin Donuts counter and order a large cup of coffee. Finally, I sit down and count the people in the station.

It is two thirty in the afternoon. There are thirteen people in the station that include: two Dunkin Donuts workers, two train terminal ticket employees and one male custodian, who just cleaned the men's room. There are a mother and daughter that appear to have just missed the bus to Logan Airport. A businessman and woman are standing while they sip coffee. Two males and one female, all of college age, are sitting down on a bench drinking bottled water. I am the thirteenth person in the terminal. Upstairs there are train tracks for the Massachusetts Bay Transit Authority and Amtrak Trains. I will go upstairs tomorrow.

It is Thursday, the fifth of September, 2002. I am at the Woburn Train Station. I stand on the upstairs platform between the two tracks for the southbound trains. On the opposite side, the northbound platform has the same two tracks setup. I and twenty other passengers get on board the 7:44 AM commuter transit train to Boston. The train is a little crowded and I have to stand. It makes stops at Winchester Center, Wedgemere and West Milford. We pass Bunker Hill

Community College, before crossing the Charles River into North Station, Boston. Bunker Hill Community College is familiar to me because I saw it in the movie *Good Will Hunting*. The train ride takes twenty-seven minutes.

Inside North Station, Boston, I see the orange colored subway line directions on a far wall. I follow the crowd out of the building and cross the street. I walk up some stairs and enter the subway station. At the token booth I buy six tokens for a buck apiece. The subway platforms are cleaner here than in New York City. The subway train arrives in a few minutes. The car is crowded and I stand. I get off this train at the Downtown Crossing Station.

I have a subway map and a map for downtown Boston. I walk a block and see the Arch Street sign. After walking a few more blocks, I enter a tall building. The second Boston firm is Manchester Automated Robotics. This is their business office in downtown Boston. The main plant for Manchester Automated Robotics is located in New Hampshire. The priority area of study at Automated Robotics is to develop systems for drug screening and vaccine production.

Mr. Seghar Bangalore is speaking to me now. He is a young version of my uncle in California. He is the same height and structure as my uncle. The facial features, small nose and good ears are similar on both men. Their skin color is tan and hair color black. The eye color is different. My uncle has blue eyes and Seghar has brown eyes. Both have the same hard working, aggressive personality. Seghar is not wearing a wedding band. A picture of a pretty, blue-eyed blond is on his desk.

Seghar says, "I, Scotty, Danny, Louis and Mario Francolone are forming a new corporation. Do you know that Mario is located in Memphis, Tennessee?"

"Yes," I answer.

"Do you have all the documents from Danny and Louis?"

"Yes, I do."

Then he says, "How do Danny and Louis like the army?"

"They actually enjoy being in the army," I answer.

"When will you see them again?"

"They will have leave around Christmas."

Seghar continues speaking, "As the agent for L&J incorporated, you will have to sign the new corporate papers for Danny and Louis."

I ask. "When will I have to do that?"

Seghar answers, "In one month. The lawyer is drawing up the contracts now. His office is near the courthouse. Are you familiar with Boston?"

"No, this is a foreign city to me."

"Why don't you walk around Boston today and get a feel for the town. When you come to work here, you will be working in the next office." He points through the door into a medium sized room with a laptop computer on the desk.

I say, "I shall be working with Scotty on Mondays and Tuesdays. Would it be OK, if I work with you on Thursdays and Fridays?"

"Sure, that will be good. Come to the office at nine in the morning. You can leave early in the afternoon or later a night. Make up your own schedule."

"Do I need an identification tag to work in this building?"

"No," says Seghar. "Next time you enter the building, you will not have to sign in and out as a visitor. Just give them your name at the ground floor main desk. Tell them you are working for Manchester Automated Robotics. You will be listed on the computer as a consultant to the company. You will be allowed to walk into the building without any problem."

After leaving the edifice, I check my watch. It is now 10:00 AM. I start to amble around Boston. It is another beautiful day with the temperature near seventy degrees Fahrenheit. Leaving Arch Street, I cross Summer Street. I walk through a shopping area, pass a hotel and turn onto Essex Street. I continue walking on Boylston Street and circumvent the Boston Common. I see a couple of theaters, pass two large hotels and turn right on Arlington Street. There is another large hotel, The Ritz Carlton. I go straight up Newbury Street and look at the fancy shops and the rich young women. I make a right hand turn on Dartmouth Street, walk past

Commonwealth Avenue and cross a highway. I arrive at the park on the Charles River.

I can see the Massachusetts Institute of Technology with the Dome Building. Danny, Louis, Scotty, Sehgar and the guy in Tennessee, Mario Francolone all graduated from this superior university. The MIT side of the river is Cambridge.

I am sitting on a bench next to the river, reading a Boston area map. The Harvard Bridge is the next bridge west. Harvard University is over the bridge and two plus miles down the road into Cambridge.

After a brief rest, I continue walking west. Student joggers pass by, as do middle-aged walkers, cyclists and mothers' with baby strollers. The river has sailboats floating upon it. At the Harvard Bridge, I turn around and head east toward the North Train Station. There is one tall building, which stands out, on the Boston side of the river. It has a strange geometrical shape.

Now walking eastward, I see the concert shell in the park, pass a boathouse, another bridge and cross the street near the Eye and Ear Infirmary. I walk around Massachusetts General Hospital to the train station and Fleet Center.

It is 12:45 PM. I decide to have lunch at an Irish Pub. I notice they have Bass ale on tap, so I order it with my hamburger and French fries. The Irish Pubs in New York's Hell's Kitchen do not carry Bass Ale. I always order a pint of Guinness in the Hell's Kitchen pubs or whatever Irish beer is on tap.

The Boston pub, I am lunching in, has a sports atmosphere. There are pictures on the wall of Bobby Ore and Phil Esposito. They were great hockey players from the 1970's. Boston Bruin fans and Celtics fans must frequent this place before and after games at Fleet Center. The food is good. Boston is famous for the seafood restaurants. However, I am allergic to shellfish so I will not be able to eat any of the famous lobster and crab dishes.

On the train ride back to Woburn, I plan my strategy for the next few months. I will not drive into Boston. They are finishing a construction project within the city. This project is called the Big Dig. It is road and tunnel construction on

Interstate Highway 93 that cuts through the middle of downtown Boston. There are new tunnels and a bridge that have just been built. There is heavy traffic in the downtown area and I do not like city driving. I would have to pay for parking, which is more expensive in the city then in the suburb of Woburn. The train commute is easy and cheap. I like to walk in cities. Boston is a historic city and there will be plenty of sites to see. When the weather gets cold, I will take the subway more and walk less. I have not noticed any watcher, observing me. However, I will be careful of the germ spreaders on the trains.

Up in Woburn, I must learn to drive the back roads near the new apartment. I also need to find a local supermarket, gas station and inexpensive restaurants. I do not intend to do much cooking. However, it will be necessary to buy food stables like: coffee, tea, milk, sugar, bread, eggs, ketchup, salt and pepper.

On my drive back from the Woburn train station, I follow a map, take a back road and find a Super Stop and Shop food market. In the parking lot, a car passes playing loud rock music. It is Joan Jett on the radio. I hear the words, "With the stereo on."

At the apartment in the evening, I turn on the television. There are seven HBO channels. The cable television schedule shows the same movies repeated, over and over again, on each of the channels. The comedy channel is different and has some of the original HBO comedy half hour shows.

I am watching an Arnold movie, *Kindergarten Cop*. The heroine of the movie is hiding in a small town. I think to myself, "This is a big mistake." A person should never hide out in a small town. The town's people always know who is a new resident.

The best place to disappear is a big city. It is easy to get lost in any city with a large public transportation system. New York and Boston are examples of cities that are great places to hide. When you know what to do, it is extremely difficult to be followed in these cities.

   In New York City, Penn Station, the Port Authority Bus Terminal and Grand Central Station are good places to go when you are being followed. You can jump onto a train, subway, bus or taxi almost immediately. Department stores like Macys and Bloomingdale's are good places too. Any location with lots of exits and people, are areas where you can become lost in a crowd. You should wear sunglasses and a hat. You should travel with a backpack. The contents of the backpack should include: a toothbrush, toothpaste, Swiss Army knife, bottled water, change of undergarments, a book, a nylon carry bag, a different style and colored jacket, another type of hat and sneakers. You can quickly change, your hat and jacket and place the backpack into the carry bag. You need to carry cash to purchase a ticket for a train or a bus. Because there are cameras at most bus and train terminals, it is best to wear a baseball cap and sunglasses to cover your face. A real desperado should have other identification. If you show a ticket clerk a driver's license with your picture on it, and a false name and address, they are not going to know if the license is real or fake. You must always pay cash. Credit cards are traced easily. A book is necessary for a long train or bus ride to another state. You will need something to read to occupy your mind. If you have a cell phone, turn it off and do not use it. Cell phones contain global positioning devices and you can be tracked within fifty meters. The World Trade Center was a good place to get lost in but it is not there anymore.
   I watch the Arnold movie a while longer, lose interest and fall asleep.
   Friday morning, the sixth of September, at 9:00 AM, I return to the Best Western Hotel and park in the lot. Lake Quannapowitt is nearby and I run around the lake. The circumference of the lake is a little more than three miles. It takes me thirty- three minutes to complete the run. The running path is the sidewalk and there are parked cars and moving vehicles on the street. I must be careful running around this lake. I will check the hilly area near my apartment and see if I can run there.

I now drive the back streets from the town of Wakefield to Woburn. I am looking for a diner. I cannot find any. There are a number of coffee and donut shops, including Dunkin Donuts. There is a McDonald's in the Woburn Mall. There are decent appearing, Chinese, Mexican, American and Italian restaurants. These restaurants are open for lunch and dinner. Driving through the towns, I realize that these roads go on a diagonal. Some of the streets crisscross the main highway. There are plenty of gasoline stations, Fleet Banks, a Staples store, Toyota Dealership, a movie complex and Gold's Gym. I grab a cup of coffee and a jelly donut at Dunkin Donuts and go home.

I am used to spending most of my time alone. I always have a book to read. Sometimes I listen to CDs or the radio. The radio stations in Massachusetts play Aerosmith constantly. In New Jersey, the local stations play Bon Jovi and Bruce Springsteen. The radio stations in New York City play everything. Hours pass by quickly when I listen to music or read a book.

I also pass time on the Internet. The Verizon Telephone Company man hooked up the phone in my apartment so I could connect to the Internet with my Dell laptop computer. I expect to receive email from both Danny and Louis. For a short period longer, I will monitor the logs and maintain the L&J Corporate website. I placed a notification on the website that L&J Incorporated will close down, December 31, 2002.

During the evening, I continue to watch some television. Sporting events and movies are what I enjoy mostly. The History Channel, Discovery Channel, Food Network and Weather Channel are good too. I do not enjoy network and cable news programs. The news organizations give opinionated, censored versions of what is happening in the world. About half of what they report is true. The other half of reporting is slanted or outright lies.

The worst programs on television are those involving politicians and political opinions. I do not believe anything the Democrats or Republicans say. I don't trust foreign heads of state or representatives from the United Nations. The personality traits of most politicians are selfish, egoistic and deceptive. Politicians have a voracious appetite for power and money. They are like dinosaurs, devouring everything in their path. I think that some politicians are actual monsters just posing as human beings.

Today is my first Saturday in Massachusetts. It is a beautiful morning. I take the train back into Boston. This time I walk along the Charles River all the way to the Boston University Bridge. According to my map there are many colleges and universities on the Boston side of the river. There are Boston University, Emerson College, Suffolk University, Tufts University, the University of Massachusetts Boston Campus and Boston College. On the Cambridge side of the river are MIT and Harvard. There are lots of other schools in the area. My apartment, in the suburbs, is not that far from Northeastern University.

There are many more people today jogging, bicycling and walking along the river. At lunchtime, I visit a pub on Commonwealth Avenue near Boston University. The patrons are local university students and their professors. I have a burger, fries and a pint of Sam Adams beer. There are television sets in strategic positions throughout the bar. I shall return to this establishment some Sundays, to watch the Patriot's football games.

On my return trip walking along the river, I stop to watch a show at the Hatch Memorial Shell. It is a rock concert. Mostly middle aged, ex-hippies are hanging out listening to the music. There are a few college students too. Since most of the audience is my age, I stay to hear a few songs. I do not know the name of this group but they are very good.

Sunday morning is another nice day. I map out a three miles jogging path near my apartment complex. I run past churches, schools and houses. Traffic is lighter on a Sunday, so I am able to run safely. However, some of the homes have dogs that are unleashed. I walk by the dogs slowly. I will avoid these homes the next time I run. When the jog is complete, I stop at the nearby Dunkin Donuts and drink a large coffee and eat a cream donut. I am going to have to change my eating habits. I

James Cage

have been eating only hamburgers and donuts since I arrived in Massachusetts.

In the afternoon I skip lunch and watch a football game at home. The score is Jets 37, Bills 31.

After the football game, I have dinner at a nearby, family style, Italian Restaurant near the Woburn Mall on Commerce Way. Because it is Sunday the establishment is crowded. I have to wait ten minutes for a table. The food is good. The spaghetti with marinara sauce, salad and bread are equivalent to a pizza takeout joint in New York City.

When I order a cup of coffee, the young waitress asks, "Where are you from?"

I answer, "New Jersey."

She says, "Where are you living in this area?"

I say, "Woburn."

She corrects my pronunciation. She says, "It is pronounced, Wu-burn." She pronounces Woburn, like the name Dr. Wu, in the song by Steely Dan. My pronunciation was "Woo-burn." I made a woo sound, like a cowboy makes pulling up his horse and saying, "Woo."

Whenever I return to this restaurant it won't be on a Sunday. I suspect that during the week there will be less people. The crowd should be different too, probably office workers and businessmen. I figure the best time to eat in this restaurant is on a weekday at 5:00 PM.

Monday, the ninth of September, is my first day of work in Wakefield. I open a file from L&J Incorporated titled "WFD Genetic Engineering." Part of this job is data entry into an Excel Spreadsheet. For most people this is boring, tedious work. But I do not mind entering numbers into a spreadsheet. The work keeps me busy. I don't have to think very much. Because I am working only two days per week in Wakefield, it will take a month for me to do this particular job. Scotty will supply more data entry work after this file is finished.

Scotty and I are the only two people occupying this office. The accounting and controller's offices are located in this section of the building. No other person enters these two rooms, or even knocks on the door. Scotty never answers the phone. The three calls that come in today go directly into the answering machine.

After lunch break I do the other part of my job. I copy computer programs, written by Louis and Danny, into the computer. These programs are written in the C programming language. As I look over the material, I can tell the programs are not complete. Scotty will finish writing these programs. The programs are written in sections. When one section is constructed properly, you check the functionality. If that part of the program works bug free, you continue onto the next part. Different people may write parts of a program. Then someone integrates the whole thing and you have your completed software program.

Scotty's company deals with genetic engineering. This program is specific to, "Enhancing the virulence of naturally sporulating organisms." From recent newspaper articles about anthrax, I know that Bacillus Anthrax is a sporulating organism. The only other sporulating organism I can think of is Clostridium Botulinum. The botulism toxin causes illness and death. I remember that from the microbiology class I took thirty years ago. I am going to have to do an Internet search on "sporulating organisms."

After completing my first day's assignment, Scotty tells me that this work has to do with Advanced Biological Warfare. This is a new government contract.

I say, "Danny and Louis are against biological warfare."

Scotty says, "That is exactly what we are doing. Danny and Louis helped create this program to thwart the creation of biological weapons. If someone develops a genetically engineered virulent organism, we create the antidote against it."

I think about the Aids virus. I wonder if that is a genetically engineered virulent organism.

When I report to WFD Genetics on Tuesday, I follow the same procedure as the preceding day. Scotty is always here to help and explain things to me.

After finishing work Tuesday, I drive to the Woburn Train Station. I take the train to Boston's North Station. I get on the orange line subway, and then at Downtown Crossing I change to the red line. I take this train to Boston's South Station. I barely catch the Amtrak's Regional Service train, departing at 6:45 PM, for New York's Penn Station.

The train arrives in New York at 10:45 PM. It is a little dangerous taking the subway late at night. So, I take a cab from Eighth Avenue to the Eighty-Third Street apartment.

Wednesday morning in New York City, I go to the local post office. I fill out a card to hold the mail for the apartment. I thought I would be able to come into New York each week. However, a one way train ride takes a minimum of three and a half hours. Most of the trains take four hours or more. A Greyhound bus or driving a car takes just as long.

Before I departed New Jersey the previous week, I told the Jersey post office to hold all my mail. I knew I would be unable to return to New Jersey every week. Now I understand that I will be unable to return to New York City each week too.

At 3:03 PM Wednesday afternoon, I take the Acela Express train, back to Boston's South Station. The train takes three and a half hours arriving at 6:33 PM. The express train costs double the regional train. I pay the train expenses out of my own pocket. I do not charge this trip to the L&J Incorporated credit card.

I eat at a pub in the South Station. I have roast beef, a baked potato, salad and a pint of Guinness. There are lots of good-looking women in this bar.

When I get to the Woburn Station, I have to pay an eight dollars parking fee for overnight and the next day.

It is Thursday's at Seghar's Company in Boston. I have the file from Danny and Louis that says, "Manchester Automated Robotics." My work is similar to the work that I do at Scotty's firm. I enter data in the morning and copy C programs in the afternoon. If I have a problem, Seghar is here to help me. I do not enter data quickly, accuracy is more important.

Seghar's Company's goal is to diagnose disease early and specifically. This is part of the Advanced Biological Warfare Program, abbreviated, ABW in the WFD and Automated

Robotics documentation. I did not know specifics about the ABW program until Scotty explained it to me on Monday.

During the four weeks period, working with Scotty and Seghar, I have maintained a good work, exercise and recreational schedule. I have managed to run or walk four times per week. In order not to waste time cooking and cleaning, I eat meals out. When I eat at my apartment, I eat fruits and vegetables. I have replaced the breakfast donuts with a soft boiled egg and whole wheat toast.

It is Wednesday morning, the second of October. I am searching the area near the Government Center on Court Street. Yesterday, Seghar gave me the new corporation contract. He told me to go over the contract with a lawyer. He asked me, "Do you need to go to New York for a lawyer or do you have one locally?"

I told him, "I have a cousin here in Boston. I shall give him a call."

After walking around in circles for half an hour, I finally find my cousin's office. There are office buildings in this area that include: the JFK Federal Building, Boston City Hall, and the Suffolk County Court House. His law office is in a large building on Cambridge Street.

My cousin Paul is a graduate of Boston University. He attended law school in Pennsylvania. He returned to Boston a few years ago to set up private practice. He is twenty years younger than I am and unmarried. Paul is a big man. He is six feet tall, two hundred pounds, blue eyes, and blond hair.

Paul has a medium size office. There is a secretary at the front desk. I have just made the 10:00 AM appointment on time. She leads me into his office. The secretary has good legs. Paul is probably fooling around with her.

He says, "This is my legal secretary Kathy."

She waves, "Hello," and goes back to her desk.

He gives me a hug and asks. "How are you doing cousin?"

I say, "Fine, you look well. How many people do you have working for you?"

Paul replies, "I have Kathy and one paralegal. He is in school right now. When he gets his law degree, I shall make him a junior partner. He is a decent kid."

Then he says, "Let's look at the contract you told me about."

He explains to me that the papers are for the formation of an S Corporation. The name of the newly formed corporation is Molay Biotech Incorporated.

He asks, "Do you know the difference between an S Corporation and a partnership?"

"Yes, I know the difference. In a partnership the partners are liable. It depends on the type of partnership, general or limited, how much liability each partner has. The S Corporation is a better setup. The corporation is a separate entity and the individuals are not liable. The corporation is responsible for payment of debt. When it comes to paying taxes, an S corporation is like a partnership. Each individual investor pays tax on the percentage of his investment. The taxpayer uses the schedule K-1 form and pays the taxes. A taxpayer in a partnership pays individual taxes the same way."

We go over the basics of the contract. Seghar, Scott and Mario have a twenty-five percent share each. Danny and Louis individually own a twelve and one half percent share. Seghar, Scott and Mario will invest $100,000 apiece into the corporation. Louis and Danny add $50,000 apiece. Total assets invested are $400,000.

The breakdown of shares at one dollar par value per share is as follows: 100,000 shares for Scott, 100,000 shares for Seghar, 100,000 shares for Mario, 45,000 shares for Danny, 45,000 shares for Louis and 10,000 shares for me.

My cousin Paul says, "Danny and Louis cut you in for ten percent of their shares because you are their agent."

I say, "Wow, they did not have to do that."

I write an L&J Incorporated check, in the amount of $500 and give it to my cousin.

He says, "Look, I don't want to take any money from you."

I say, "This is a business expense and L&J Incorporated needs a lawyer in Massachusetts."

Paul speaks, "I'll take you to lunch. It is a nice day out. We can go for a walk."

We walk through the Boston Common, go across Charles Street, and enter the Public Gardens. We cross the next street, walk past the hotel and get onto fancy Newbury Street. We eat at an Italian restaurant. My cousin and I order the same meal: a dish of pasta, salad and a glass of Chianti. This restaurant is equivalent to a good Italian eatery in New Jersey. It cannot compare to an Italian restaurant in Manhattan, New York City.

My cousin spends some time with me. He shows me Chinatown and the Financial Center. I notice there is a World Trade Center in Boston. I did not know that. He also takes me past Paul Revere's House.

I say, "At the end of his midnight ride, didn't Paul Revere say, Woo."

My cousin laughs.

At 3:00 PM, Paul leaves me at the North Station. It was good to see him.

October, 2002

On Friday morning, the eleventh of October, I begin my drive back to New Jersey. Monday is the Columbus Day holiday. Seghar told me on Thursday to take Friday off. Scotty gave me Monday and Tuesday off. Wednesday, I can use as a travel day. One of the women who I have lunch with at Scotty's, WFD company, told me to take Interstate 90, the Massachusetts Turnpike and cut through Connecticut.

There is heavy traffic on Interstate 90 and I have to pay a toll. This ride is better than taking Interstate 95 on the coast. At Exit 9 on the turnpike, I get off and enter Interstate Highway 84. This road takes me through Hartford the capital of Connecticut. I pass the University of Connecticut in Farmington. I take Highway 84 all the way through Danbury. I know my way from here. In the 1980's, I would visit my Uncle Jerry at the Federal Penitentiary in Danbury. He was there for a couple of years on a bookmaking rap. At Danbury, I get onto Highway 684 and go south through Westchester County in New York State.

Now, I am driving on Highway 287. Traffic slows because of roadwork. I pay the toll on the New York side of the Tappan Zee Bridge. I continue my journey a few miles west, turn south and enter the Garden State Parkway into New Jersey. I arrive home after six hours of traveling. The ride was at least one half hour less than my initial ride to Boston. However, on my return trip, I have to go to New York City, so I am going to take the coast and Interstate 95.

Saturday in New Jersey, I collect my mail at the post office. I pay any bills that have arrived and mail them out. Part of the afternoon, I look out the window to see if any unmarked white vans are passing by. Thankfully, none are.

From the front window, I also watch for certain types of people that may walk by my house. I don't like it when someone in a jogging suit and in good physical condition walks by. I wonder why they are walking and not jogging. If it is a man or a woman and they are in running gear, they should be running. If they are walking, he or she is probably a watcher.

On Sunday Morning the thirteenth of October, I go for a walk on the boardwalk. I do not put on jogging gear other than sneakers. Usually on Columbus Day weekend, I run in an eighteen miles race on Long Beach Island. But I am too tired to run even five miles. I decide that this is the last time I drive from Boston to New Jersey. When I come back home for Thanksgiving, I shall take the train. The next time I drive to New Jersey, my business in Boston will be complete.

Late Monday evening, I drive into Manhattan. I sleep at the East Eighty Third Street apartment.

Tuesday, I go to the local post office on Eighty-Fifth Street near Third Avenue and pick up the mail. After returning to the apartment, I check for any correspondence from Danny and Louis. There are no letters from the boys. There is mostly junk mail and a few bills. I pay the bills. I have not received any email from the boys since August.

My next job is to visit the New York lawyer. The local number six, subway train from Eighty-Sixth Street, takes ten minutes to arrive at Thirty-Third Street. I walk the few blocks west, to the Empire State Building. The lawyer's office is on a middle floor.

The lawyer is a woman. She is a New York girl that received her law degree from Fordham University in Manhattan. Her name is Susan. Her age is forty-three years old. She has a fine figure and is five feet, five inches tall. There is a picture of a boy and girl on her desk. Like their mother, both siblings have blue eyes and brown hair. The children are one year apart. The boy is eleven and the girl is twelve years old. Susan is divorced and does not have a picture of her ex-husband.

I say, "Susan this is the file for the new company Danny and Louis are forming." I hand it to her.

She says, "I have an email from Danny." Danny says, "He and Louis will be extremely busy over the next two months. You will be hearing from them in a few weeks."

Then she asks, "Are the young couple who are leasing Danny's apartment, going to renew the lease at the end of November?"

I answer, "No, they are not. Should I keep the apartment open, so when Danny gets back in December, he can stay in his own place?"

"Yes, that's what he wants." Then Susan adds, "Are you staying at Louis's apartment?"

"Yeah I am but just for tonight, than I am leaving for Boston in the morning."

Susan says, "Too bad I am busy this evening with the kids."

"Maybe we can get together after Thanksgiving?" I ask.

"Be sure to call me." She gives me a peck on the cheek and I leave.

Susan is an Irish girl that likes Italian food. Her favorite restaurant is Divino's on Second Avenue near Eighty-First Street. We have eaten there a couple of times. I like Susan. Her fair skin always smells fresh and clean.

Two weeks have gone by since my trip to New Jersey and New York. Seghar and I are about to have dinner at a Mexican restaurant in Woburn. Scotty, Seghar and I just completed a meeting at the WFD building in Wakefield. The date is Thursday, the twenty-fourth of October.

Seghar says, "How's the food here?"

"Not bad, try the burritos. They are pretty good."

He orders the beef burritos and a pint of Bohemia beer on tap. I order the same.

He says, "What time does your train leave for Memphis tomorrow?"

I answer, "The Amtrak train leaves from South Station to Chicago, tomorrow afternoon at 1:00 PM. I'll be in Chicago, Saturday morning. Then I will have to kill ten hours in Chicago before the train leaves for Memphis. I'll arrive in Memphis, Tennessee Sunday, the twenty-seventh."

Seghar asks, "Is Memphis a foreign city to you?"

"No, I've been in Memphis. Saint Jude Hospital, Graceland and Beal Street are places familiar to me in Memphis."

After I pay for dinner, I drop Seghar off at the Woburn train station. He still lives in Cambridge not far from where he went to school.

As Seghar exits the car he asks, "Are you going to park in long term parking for two weeks, when you take the train into Boston tomorrow?"

"No, it is cheaper to take a taxi then park for two weeks at the Woburn Train Station."

He says, "Have a nice trip."

I answer, "See you in a few weeks."

Memphis, Tennessee

It is 7 AM, Sunday morning, the twenty-seventh of October, 2002. I had an extra hour sleep because daylight savings time just ended. I have arrived in Memphis. The train station is desolate. I am nervous and tumble down an entire flight of concrete stairs. I land on my luggage. My luggage consists of a backpack and a medium size carry bag. Both the backpack and carry bag are stuffed with clothes. I don't have a scratch on me after the fall.

I leave the Memphis Train Station and walk across the empty street to the Arcadia Restaurant. Luckily, the diner is open.

I ask the waitress, "Do you have a telephone number for a taxi cab?"

She writes down the number on a napkin and gives it to me. I call the taxi service from my cell phone. The cab is in front of the diner to pick me up in a few minutes.

I ask the driver, "How did you get here so fast?"

He drives us around the corner and points to the cab company. I know where I am. Beale Street is about six blocks to the north in downtown, Memphis.

A song sings in my brain, "Just about a mile from the Mississippi Bridge." I can see the Mississippi River and the bridge to the southwest. The bridge in the song is the Memphis-Arkansas-bridge, which is Interstate 55. The bridge's original name was the E.H. Crump Bridge. It was the first bridge I ever drove across the Mississippi River.

About one mile north is the Hernando De Soto Bridge. It crosses the river at Interstate 40. I don't think the Hernando De Soto Bridge was built until 1973. I have crossed that bridge many times.

Many moons ago, The Chickasaw Indians inhabited this area when Hernando De Soto explored the Mississippi Basin in the 1540's. James Winchester, John Overton and Andrew Jackson founded the City of Memphis in 1819. Andrew Jackson is my favorite United States President.

The cab driver continues the ride and turns south to enter Interstate 240. We are driving to East Memphis. The ride is twelve miles. It takes about a half hour to arrive at the La Quinta Inn. I have a suite here. Because it is early in the morning, I wait an hour before the rooms are ready. The hotel has a free breakfast buffet. I have coffee and whole, wheat toast.

It is Monday. I am driving my rented, gray, Chevrolet, heading west on Poplar Avenue. The ride is a bit more than five miles and ends near the University of Memphis on Central Avenue.

I am inside a three-story building. Presently, I am speaking to Mario Francolone. He is the owner and president of Payen Nanotechnology. There is a black and white photo of a very pretty girl on his desk.

James Cage

Mario Francolone was born in Philadelphia. He is a large structured young man. He stands six feet three inches tall and weighs two hundred thirty pounds. He has a dark complexion, dark hair and eyes. He did his undergraduate work at the University of Pennsylvania and graduate work at MIT.

He explains, "A nanometer is one billionth of a meter. Nanotechnology is the engineering of tiny machines. Payen Nanotechnology builds nanorobots that perform a specific task. We research the transportation capacities of proteins. Under ultraviolet light a two nanometers dot glows green and a five nanometers dot glows red. These two quantum dots show colored trails when injected into cells inside Petri dishes. Do you understand the concept?"

"Yes," I answer. "The colored trails make the proteins easy to track." I think of the colored subway lines in Boston that are also easy to track.

Then I say, "Mario, are you related to that greatest, Italian American, Benjamin Francolone?"

"Absolutely," he answers.

I know that I shall get along really well with Mario.

Then Mario enthusiastically states, "In the future, these nanorobots may be able to cure disease caused by genetic deficiencies, by altering the deoxyribonucleic acid molecules."

"Woo," I think.

My work at Payen Nanotechnology is a bit different. The computer work involves the usual data entry. However, I am running statistical tests. I run a Paired Two Sample Means T-Test on the data. This is a parametric test. I also run the numbers through the Wilcoxon Matched-Pairs Signed-Ranks Test, which is a non-parametric measurement.

The difference between a parametric test and a nonparametric test is the following. A parametric test makes the assumption of a normal population distribution. This is a bell shaped curve. A nonparametric test does not make an assumption about a population distribution. Computer software easily calculates the P-values for these tests. A P-value measures evidence against the null hypothesis. The smaller the P-value, the higher the probability is that we should reject the null hypothesis.

The null hypothesis states that two sample means are equal. The computer I am working on has high, speed Internet access. So I type into an Internet search, null hypothesis +definition. I want to be sure I understand what I am doing, so I read the entire null hypothesis definition.

At WFD Genetic Engineering, Manchester Automated Robotics and Payen Nanotechnology, I work only with the principal owner of the firm. I do not work with any other employee. When I come into contact with other employees during lunchtime, someone always asks me, "What is my job at the company."

I answer truthfully. "I am a temporary employee. My job is data entry."

In the four years I worked for Danny and Louis at L&J Incorporated I was the only employee. They never brought in temporary help.

On Friday evening, the first of November, All Saints Day, Mario takes me to dinner. We are in a good country restaurant. The waitress comes over and Mario says to her, "I'd like a southern fried steak, mashed sweet potatoes and turnip greens; oh, and a bottle of Budweiser beer to drink."

I say, "I'll have the same."

He says, "Do you know what southern fried steak is?"

"Yeah, in Texas it's called chicken fried steak. In New York City you would call southern fried steak and turnip greens, a veal cutlet and broccoli rabe."

"It's just like Italian food," says Mario.

Then he asks, "Where did Louis and Danny find a guy like you?"

I answer, "A number of years ago, they placed an advertisement in the employment section of the newspaper. I answered the advertisement and they gave me the job."

I continue, "Originally, I thought I would be doing general bookkeeping and accounting work. But I started doing some of the scientific stuff too. Danny and Louis were traveling all the time doing consulting work. They needed someone to do the data entry and statistical applications."

Mario says, "Danny, Louis, Scotty, Seghar and I have been working on this project for quite a while. I will encrypt all the data. All of us have the encryption code keys to unscramble any data that we shall transfer amongst ourselves. No one else in any of our firms will see the completed material. Our employees work on sections of the research, so they will not understand the totality of the project. Do you know what is going on?"

"Yes, if there is a biological attack in the future, you want to develop methods to rapidly diagnose the causative biological agent. The agent can be bacteria, virus or a toxin. By genetic engineering, you'll alter the DNA or RNA of the bacteria or virus, so it does not cause any infectious disease or epidemic." Then I say, "You will also want to have the capability of manufacturing a drug or vaccine against the causative agent. The project is to stop the germ spreaders."

"That's it," says Mario.

The waitress brings our dinner. The food is very good.

Late Saturday morning the second of November, All Soul's Day or the Day of the Dead in Mexico, I drive south on US Highway 61 to the casinos in Tunica, Mississippi. It is a forty miles drive that takes seventy minutes. I park the rented Chevy at the Gold Strike Casino. The actual location of this casino is Casino Center Drive Robbinsville, Mississippi. I explore the four casinos in this area: the Gold Strike, Grand, Horseshoe and Sheraton.

At lunchtime, in the Gold Strike's fast food, restaurant section, I have a piece of pecan pie and coffee. When I am in the south, I always enjoy a piece of pecan pie.

I need to be careful how I pronounce the word coffee. When I was seventeen years old, I visited my uncle in Los Angeles, California. We went to a coffee shop. When I ordered coffee, the waitress said, "You must be from the east." I had pronounced the word coffee, "caw-fee."

Years later in late June of 1996, I was driving through Fort Worth, Texas and stopped at McDonald's. I ordered a cup of coffee. The order taker, a young girl about nineteen years old said, "Are you from New York."

"Yes," I answered.

Then she said, "Have you ever read the book *Sleepers*?"

"No, I never heard of it."

The young girl then said, "Read it, you'll enjoy the book."

Eventually I did read the book *Sleepers* and enjoyed it. The girl was correct.

There are a number of casinos spread over several miles throughout Tunica, Mississippi. I take a shuttle bus and visit most of them. I visit the Hollywood, Harrah's, Sam's Town, and Bally's. The casinos have replaced some cotton fields. I think of the song lyrics, "Those old cotton fields back home."

At the entrance to Sam's Town Casino a sign reads, "No guns allowed." I never saw a sign like that in the Atlantic City casinos or the Las Vegas gambling palaces.

After my shuttle bus ride, I return to the Gold Strike Casino. I watch the poker players. They take poker very seriously in Mississippi. I would never sit and play poker here. I pass the time playing the poker slot machines. I lose twenty dollars in forty-five minutes and listen to the people in the casino. Most of them are from Tennessee, Mississippi, Arkansas, Louisiana and Texas.

What I like most about the Tunica casino is listening to the blues band and drinking a few beers. There is no charge for the beers and I leave the bartender ten bucks. As I watch the southern woman dance around in blue jeans, I keep my mouth shut. I enjoy the evening. At midnight, I drive back to my hotel in Memphis.

After a week at Mario's company I receive an email from Danny. Danny says, "Louis and I are doing fine. Hope the work is going smoothly."

My last night in Memphis is Friday, the eighth of November. I have an early dinner with Mario and his girlfriend Nancy. We are at Ruth Chris's steak house, near to my hotel. We all order steak and wine.

Nancy says, "Is *The Godfather* your favorite movie? It is Mario's favorite movie."

James Cage

"No," I say. "My favorite movie is *The Usual Suspects*. Do you know the movie?"

"Oh yes," she says. "Gabriel Byrne and Kevin Spacey star in it."

Mario says, "What is your favorite Italian, gangster movie?"

"*Goodfellas*," I answer.

"Did you grow up with guys like that back east?" Mario asks.

"Yes, I did."

Nancy, the movie buff, asks, "What is your favorite foreign film."

I answer, *The Night Porter*, starring Charlotte Rampling and Dirk Bogard." I also think about a comedy starring Ugo Tognazzi, but I don't mention it.

"I have never seen it," she says. "Is that about a Nazi concentration camp survivor and a former SS Officer?"

"Yes." I don't tell her that it is an Italian film by Liliana Cavani, made in 1974. The title in Italian is *Portiere di Notte*.

Then I say, "You guys may be able to rent a video of *The Night Porter*."

Nancy says, "I have seen Charlotte Rampling in the movie *The Verdict*, with Paul Newman. What movies has Dirk Bogard starred in?"

I answer, "He was in *The Damned* with Charlotte Rampling and *Death in Venice*. I did not like those movies very much."

A few hours later, at 11:00 PM, I board the Memphis train to Chicago. It is a warm evening and clear night. All the *Twilight Zone People* are on the train. I do not worry about the *Twilight Zone People*. They are not the watchers.

Back in Boston

On Veteran's Day Monday, November 11, 2002, I receive an email from Louis.

Louis's email says, "Danny and I have completed this set of language courses in California. We are currently stationed at Fort Bragg, North Carolina. We are in training and are attached to the 519th Military Intelligence Battalion. This group provides interrogation of enemy prisoners of war. The 519th also does long range reconnaissance, surveillance and counter intelligence support to the XVIII Airborne Corp."

I email back, "That sounds like extremely interesting work and a terrific assignment."

On Wednesday, the twenty-seventh of November, I return to New Jersey from Boston for Thanksgiving. I took the train instead of driving. I celebrate the holiday with my cousin Nicky and his family.

Saturday morning the thirtieth of November, I take a New Jersey Transit Train to New York City. I spend Saturday evening with Susan. I am glad I did not forget to call her.

The next day Sunday, the first of December, I return to Boston on the Acela Express Train. With the exception of the two weeks I spent in Memphis and a couple of trips to New Jersey and New York, I have been in Boston since the beginning of September. The weather has become much colder through the month of November.

The date is Thursday December 19, 2002. I am preparing to leave Boston for New Jersey. Both Scotty and Seghar offer me a job.

They say, "Danny and Louis will be in the service for a few more years and there will not be any real work for you to do in New York. Why don't you stay here and work with us?"

I thank them both but turn down the job offer.

I reflect on the time I spent in Boston. I never finished the book I was reading about forensic accounting. I only went to see one movie, *City by the Sea*, starring Robert Di Niro. The movie setting was Long Beach, New York but much of the film was shot in Asbury Park, New Jersey. Most of my evenings in

Massachusetts were spent, searching the Internet. I also listened to music and watched movies on HBO. Because of the cold weather and frequent snow, I had to join Gold's Gym and run on a treadmill throughout the months of November and December.

I enjoyed Boston. The people were nice and the food was good. I got to visit the campus at the Massachusetts Institute of Technology. I also saw the Boston University Campus. I never made it over to Harvard or Boston College. The entire time I was in Massachusetts, I did not notice any watchers watching me, or unmarked white vans following me.

New York/New Jersey

It is Monday, the twenty-third of December. At a local Manhattan pub, I am having an early dinner with Louis and Danny. We are having hamburgers, French fries and Bass Ale. They both look strong and healthy. They talk about army life and say they are intelligence analysts. At some point in time they will be translators. After more than a year in the service they are still second lieutenants.

They ask me to spend Christmas with them. I know they have girlfriends in the city and they have been invited to have Christmas Eve and Christmas Day with the girls. I tell them I am having the holiday in New Jersey with my cousin's family.

Danny is staying at his West Side condominium. I will lease the condo again, after he returns to North Carolina in January 2003.

The coming year, I will also lease Louis's Eighty-Third Street apartment. There will be no need for me to remain in New York City. I can always take the train from New Jersey into Manhattan and return back to New Jersey. When necessary I can spend the night in a Manhattan hotel.

Danny says, "Thanks for doing such a fine job for us in New England and Memphis."

Louis adds, "Our associates liked you and said you worked extremely hard to complete all the data files."

I say, "I like to keep busy. I enjoyed doing the work and I learned a lot of stuff. It was nice to live in Boston and visit Tennessee."

Danny says, "Since you're not having Christmas with us, why don't you come over for New Year's Eve."

I answer. "You guys enjoy your New Year with your old friends and some of your new army buddies. We can get together after the New Year holiday. We can take care of business and go out to dinner too."

It is Monday January 6, 2003. The new, year has started. I am at the lawyer's office in the Empire State Building. Danny, Louis, Susan and I are going over formal legal documents.

Susan will dissolve L&J Incorporated. When I do the corporate taxes for L&J Incorporated it will be the final filing.

Danny and Louis are now partners in the new company, Molay Biotech Incorporated, which is registered in Massachusetts. My cousin Paul, the lawyer in Boston, will correspond with Susan, the lawyer in New York, pertaining to Molay Biotech's legal affairs.

A trust fund, The L&J Living Trust Fund, is being set up. The firm in Silicon Valley, California has been notified that any checks written as payment for the L&J Incorporated computer program should be written to The L&J Living Trust Fund.

All assets of Louis and Daniel are being placed into the trust fund. These include: Daniel's Westside condo, Louis's Eastside apartment and all prior corporate assets from L&J Incorporated. All money earned from Molay Biotech Incorporated, will go into the trust. Danny and Louis have placed all their bond holdings and savings into the trust fund. They do not own any stocks.

When the stock market crashed in the year 2000, investors lost seven trillion dollars' worth of assets. This was a staggering amount of money that was barely mentioned in the press. Although I am an extremely careful investor, I lost twenty-two thousand dollars. Daniel and Louis lost nothing. They had all their money invested in five and ten year United States Treasury Notes. I knew that these guys were very, very smart.

Danny and Louis are the main beneficiaries of the new living trust fund. If they become deceased, Susan and I as co-executors of the trust will distribute the fund's assets as stated in the trust's documents.

Louis and Danny offer me a full salary for the next two years.

I say, "No, you guys have paid me more than enough money. I'll take care of the accounting records, bank accounts, taxes and rental of the apartments. Also, I will contact your business partners when necessary. I know you have expenses provided for me in the trust fund. That is enough money for me."

In the late afternoon, Susan, Danny, Louis and I have an early dinner at Divino's Italian Restaurant on Second Avenue. We have two bottles of the house recommended red wine, a Merlot. I make sure I pay the bill.

On Friday, the seventeenth of January, Louis takes the train to my home in New Jersey. Daniel flew back to North Carolina from LaGuardia Airport on Thursday the sixteenth.

Saturday morning the eighteenth of January, I drive Louis to Fort Dix and McGuire Air Force Base in New Jersey. Before 911, Fort Dix was an open base. However, after the attacks, all entrances to the base are guarded. When I drop Louis at the gate he says, "Have you ever been on this base before?"

I answer, "Yes, I have. There is a federal penitentiary on this base. Over the years I have visited friends here."

I wish Louis luck. We shake hands. I turn the car around and leave. Louis is headed overseas. He did not tell me where he is going, nor did I ask him.

Afghanistan

The war in Afghanistan has been going on since October 2001. Louis is trained in Dari, an Afghani official language. Obviously, Afghanistan is his overseas assignment. By reading some books and doing searches on the Internet, I learn some facts about Afghanistan.

Afghanistan is about the size of Texas. It is a land locked country. It is mostly a mountainous land with two arid plains. It is bordered by Iran on the west and part of the southwest. Pakistan borders Afghanistan on the east and most of the south. Countries on the northern border from west to east include: Turkmenistan, Uzbekistan, Tajikistan and China. There are approximately thirty million Afghans. The main ethnic groups are the Pashtu and the Tajik. Other tribal groups are: the Hazara, Uzbek, Amik, Turkmen and Baloch. These tribes all speak in their own dialect. Afghan Persian or Dari and Pashtu are the official languages. The Dari language is similar to Farsi, the Persian-Iranian language. About eighty percent of Afghanis are Sunni Muslim and seventeen percent are Shia Muslim.

Opium is the main export from this impoverished land. The tribes in the north grow the poppy flower. Opium is extracted from the poppy. There are laboratories in Afghanistan that process raw opium into heroin. The source of eighty percent of the heroin in Europe comes from Afghanistan. In the 1960's and 70's, the raw opium from Afghanistan was shipped to laboratories in Marseilles and Sicily then processed into heroin. The heroin was sent to Europe and North America.

This is the time line to follow on Afghanistan. In 1978 there is a communist coup in Afghanistan. The Soviet Union controls a puppet government in Kabul. Kabul is the capital city of the country. In June 1978, the Mujahedeen movement is born to rid the country of the communists.

During the 1980's, the Soviet Union fights a long drawn out war in Afghanistan. Eventually the Mujahedeen defeat the Soviets. The United States, through the Central Intelligence Agency, helps the Mujahedeen. The CIA supplies guns, money and training to the Mujahedeen. Osama Bin Laden, his radical Islamic soldiers, the Northern Alliance, and other Muslim groups are recipients of this aid. Iran and Pakistan also are involved in the internal affairs of Afghanistan. The Soviet invaders are defeated and withdraw from Afghanistan on February 15, 1989.

In 1992, the Mujahedeen sets up an Islamic state and the ruling Islamic Jihad Council. In 1994, because of intense friction among the nation's different ethnic groups, the Taliban militia seizes power in Afghanistan.

The Taliban are an extreme Islamic fundamentalist group. In 1996, the Taliban force women to be fully veiled. Women are no longer allowed to work. Men must grow beards. Buzkashi, the Afghan national sport is outlawed.

I saw a version of Buzkashi in the movie, *The Man Who Would Be King*. The story is from a Rudyard Kipling novel. The movie has Sean Connery and Michael Caine as the main protagonists. In the sport Buzkashi, a head is put into a bag and placed in the center of a field. Two opposing teams on horseback, bang the head around until a team scores a goal. The modern day version of Buzkashi uses a headless, goat carcass instead of the head of an enemy. The game is obviously great fun.

Some middle class Afghans leave the country when the Taliban assert authority. Many of these Afghanis move to the San Francisco, California area. I assume some of these immigrants teach Dari, Pashtu and other Afghani tribal dialects to military personnel at the language school in Monterrey.

In 2001, the Taliban destroy ancient historical statues in the Kabul museum. They destroy historical sites in Ghazni and blow up giant Bamiyan Buddhas built in the fifth century. I remember seeing the Buddhist shrine destroyed on television.

On March 19, 2003 I receive an email from Louis.

Louis says, "In two days, on the twenty-first of March, the Afghani celebrates New Years. I am sending this email from Bagram Airfield about one and a half hours ride from Kabul. When I left New Jersey in January, I flew to Ramstein Airbase in Germany. Before arriving in Afghanistan, I stopped in Turkey and Kyrgyzstan. Presently, I am stationed at Bagram. The weather is not as cold as last month. The winter weather has been dreary, miserable, cold, and snowy. I have had two assignments in Kabul with the International Security Force near the US Embassy. Most of my time is spent reading documents. My Dari language skills are improving. I am also learning Pashtu. My fellow soldiers and airmen are in good spirits. The weather is supposed to turn hot and dry in the summer. I prefer the warmer weather."

Louis continues, "I will have fifteen days leave around Christmas. Hopefully, Danny will have leave about the same time. Are the New York apartments leased for the month of January 2004?"

My reply email states, "Both apartments are leased through January, 2004. You and Danny can stay with me in New Jersey. Take care of yourself."

<u>Iraq</u>

In early February, 2003, I had received a call from Danny. He said he would be going overseas and I would not be hearing from him for a while. He did not have any contact with Louis after he returned to North Carolina.

On March 20, 2003 the United States, Great Britain and a few other allies invade Iraq. Danny is a special, forces intelligence officer. He has Arabic language training. I assume he is part of the invasion into Iraq.

Through the months of April, May and June of 2003, I only receive short emails from Danny and Louis. They just say they are safe and working hard.

It is Monday, the twenty-first of July, 2003. I receive an email from Danny. It is the first time I have heard from him in a month.

Danny writes, "I am sending this email from the Green Zone in Baghdad. I have been in Iraq since late March. The first stop I made in the Middle East was Qatar. I was stationed there for a bit more than two months. I have been with the 82nd Airborne in Ramadi and Anbar Province."

He continues, "The climate in July is unbelievable hot and dry. It must be close to 130 degrees Fahrenheit. Do you have any idea how miserably hot this is?"

Actually I did have an idea of the heat. Many years ago I was in San Luis Potosi, Mexico. It was 126 degrees Fahrenheit. I had to stop at a hotel because the car I was driving would overheat. The hotel room had a fan. There was no air conditioning. I could only rest on the bed and drink water. I was headed for Laredo, Texas. I left San Luis Potosi before 4 AM, when the air temperature had cooled down. I was stuck in that heat for only one day. It must be difficult to be in heat like that for many months.

The rest of Danny's email is standard Department of Defense email that can be found on the Internet. The DOD email states: *"The sand gets into everything. It jams the M16 rifles. I have a HK military .45 caliber pistol. It is a reliable weapon. The young soldiers like firing the M240 .308 caliber machine gun and the M2 .50 caliber heavy machine gun. Those large weapons stop the enemy. Some of the special operations guys use the Barrett .50 caliber sniper rifle. They say it is a terrific weapon. The marine snipers use the M24 .308 sniper rifle. The enemy uses AK-47's rifles and light machine guns. The enemy is no match for our trained troops and fire power. The rocket, propelled grenade is used against us with success. The RPG is easy for someone to learn how to handle. It maims and kills. The improvised explosive device, IED, is the main killer of our soldiers and marines. Iraqi civilians, police and soldiers are wounded more from the improvised explosive devices than anything else. The enemy wires artillery shells together and detonates them with a cell phone. These explosives blow up our vehicles. It is dangerous to drive."*

Danny's long email continues. "The enemy comes from Syria, Saudi Arabia and Jordan, as well as Iraq. We have captured prisoners who do not speak Arabic. They speak Farsi and are from Iran. We have even captured insurgents from Chechnya. However with all the chaos, the moral of the soldiers and marines is high. My tour will be up Christmas time. See you then."

My email reply is, "Louis and you are staying with me in New Jersey for Christmas. Be safe."

I follow the war on the Internet. I see terrorists behead innocent human beings. I do not watch network news programs. I occasionally watch cable news. The networks and cable news organizations censor the war. The Internet does not censor anything. As time passes, I stop watching the videos of the killings. These videos give me nightmares.

James Cage

Back In Time

I have a nightmare. I wake up in a cold sweat. Since, I am
unable to sleep, I go back in time.

It is early 1980's. I have an easy job that pays lots of money.
I am in Venice, Italy. I am not particularly fond of Venice.
The Italian dialect spoken in Venice is different. They speak
with a slight lisp. I don't like the smell of the canals. The
place reminds me of Seaside Heights, New Jersey. Both places
are a bit sinister.

I am waiting to meet a man that I know, to give him a
package. He is called the Welshman.

I meet him in front of a hotel near the train station in Venice.
I give the Welshman the package.

He says, "Thanks."

I leave.

At dusk, I decide to take a walk before dinner. I turn down an
alley. I have never noticed any cars in Venice. I have only
seen boats in the canals. An unmarked white van pulls in front
of me. Suddenly, I get cracked on the right ear with a heavy
object. I literally see stars before I pass out.

When I regain consciousness, I am in a gray room. There are
four masked men in the room with me. My head hurts very
badly. I have trouble breathing. Two guards have wrapped a
wet towel over my mouth and nose. They have been drowning
me a little at a time, by dipping my head into a large, tub of
water.

The interrogator asks me, "Who sent you?"

I answer, "The Controller."

He says, "What is his name?"

I answer, "The Controller."

"The name on the driver's license and credit cards. Is this
your name?"

"Yes," I say. I realize that the Interrogator's accent is
American.

He says, "What is your business in Venice?"

I answer, "I am visiting a friend."

Then he says, "What is your friend's name?"

I answer, "The Welshman."

This goes on for a while. One of the guards takes a cigarette and burns my left foot with it. Then the Interrogator begins the questions again. The torture goes on a while longer.

The fourth masked guy has been watching. He comes over. The two torturer guards pull my pants off. The fourth guy takes out a scalpel.

I wake up in a small private hospital. My left foot is bandaged. Gauss is plugged into my right ear. I look down.

A doctor walks into the room. He says, "Don't worry. You will be fine. I put some stitches in."

I say, "What happened."

The Doc says, "A surgeon circumcised you. You are completely intact."

I thanked the Doc and God too.

In the evening the Welshman enters into my room. I ask him, "What happened."

He says, "There is a tracking device on one of your credit cards. The Controller and I realized you were in trouble when we locked in on you. You were not at the hotel. You were in one location for over six hours. That would be too long to be in a restaurant, even in Italy."

The Welshman speaks some more, "When we came into the place, you were out cold. There were two men. The Controller and I killed them both."

I say, "There were four of them." I figure the Welshman and Controller got the two torturer guards. That would leave the Interrogator and the Surgeon.

The Welshman asks, "Did you tell them anything?"

I report, "No." Then I add, "If you ever find out about the other two guys, let me know."

"Can you describe them in any way?" he asks.

I answer, "I never saw their faces. The Interrogator has an American accent. He speaks the way a television newsman does anywhere in the United States. The other guy, the Surgeon did not speak. He just cut and snipped." I continue, "They are both your height, about six feet tall. They are thinly built. Their body odor is different, not like that of Europeans. They both smelled like soap."

The Welshman says, "You'll be OK."

"Yeah, I guess so. This wasn't the easy job, I thought it would be. I thought I was just the messenger, or perhaps a decoy, or something."

The Welshman says, "The Controller will take care of you."

The Controller still takes care of me. He sends me one thousand dollars every month. The check is from a trust fund located in Bermuda. From time to time, I make a delivery for him. The Controller has paid me lots of money over the years.

I was never completely OK after the incident in Venice. The crack on the right ear busted the eardrum. I have to sleep with two pillows propped up. If I lay flat, I get dizzy. My right eyelid droops a bit. It is slightly lower than the left eyelid. The eyelids used to be equal. I also have a little nip on the underside of my private part. My left foot healed perfectly. When I think about this incident, I know I am lucky.

Back to Present

It is Thursday, December 25, 2003. Louis, Danny and I are having Christmas dinner together. They are both leaner and that all American bright, glow surrounding each of them is tinged with a few red spots. They look like a couple of Vietnam veterans I knew many, years ago. The souls of those Vietnam vets and the souls of Louis and Danny are the same.

We are having, baked ziti, sausage, meatballs, and salad for dinner. We are drinking red wine and club soda.

During Christmas dinner, I ask Louis to explain, the Persian language to me.

He says, "The Persian language is an Indo-European language. It is different from Arabic. Originally the language was written in Pahlavi Script, from right to the left. The language is now written in Arabic symbols from right to left."

I ask, "What is Pahlavi Script?"

Louis answers, "Pahlavi was an Iranian language used in Persia during the reign of the Sassanids."

I say, "I better look up Sassanids on the Internet."

He continues, "The Iranian Persian language is named Farsi-Dari. The Persian language in Afghanistan and Pakistan is called Dari. In Tajikistan and Uzbekistan the language is called Tajik. The differences would be like someone from England speaking to an American, or an American talking to an Australian. The people who speak formal Persian can all understand one another."

Danny chimes in, "Standard Arabic, the Arabic on Al-Jezzara, can be understood throughout the Middle East. But the dialects are different in all the countries. Iraqi Arabic is different from Egyptian Arabic. The Arabic spoken in Lebanon and Syria is slightly different. Moroccan Arabic is not the quite same as the other dialects. Some of the tribes have dialects that only tribal members can understand."

I write this down for Danny.

احنرس المسا مع جرثوم عن ال قطار

I ask, "What does this mean?"

Danny answers, "Reading from right to left. The letters are: alif, Haa, nuun, raa, a space, sinn. The first word means 'Beware.' The second word is: alif, laam, miim, sinn, alif, a space, miim, ayn, which means 'The Traveler.' The third word starts with a j or jimm, raa, a space, thaa, waa, a space and ends in m, or mimm. I think it means 'Germ.' The fourth word's spelling: ayn, nuun means 'On.' The fifth word is: alif, laam, which means 'The.' The last word spells, qaaf, Taa, alif, raa, 'Train'."

Danny asks, "Where did you get this from?"

I answer, "From an Arabic website on the Internet."

Danny says, "Your script is pretty damn good."

I say, "It is easy just to copy stuff."

I never tell Danny and Louis that I was once interested in comparative religions. I studied a little Arabic on my own. These words came to me in a dream. If I dreamed them up they could not possibly be grammatically correct.

I change the subject and say, "On December 13, 2003 the former President of Iraqi was captured. Since you two soldiers are intelligence officers, how did the army finally capture Saddam Hussein?"

Danny answers, "Someone ratted him out for money."

I say, "How come he was not shot immediately. His sons were killed in battle."

Danny says, "The politicians wanted him taken alive. They want a public trial to show the world the atrocities he committed."

I don't say anything. I think, to take the President of Iraq alive is a mistake. I remember watching on television, the uprising in Romania in December, 1989. The insurgents quickly executed the socialist dictator Nicholae Ceausescu and his wife. That is the way to do it.

The day after Christmas, Danny and Louis rent a burgundy, Ford Taurus and drive to Boston. Their business partner Mario flies to Logan Airport from Memphis. Danny, Louis and Mario will meet Seghar and Scotty at the Four Seasons Hotel in downtown Boston. The boys tell me they will return to New Jersey with the financial statements of Molay Biotech Incorporated. My job is to go over the statements and do the 2003 taxes. I already know the government contract is for two million dollars for year one, December, 2002 to December, 2003. And there is a new contract with the government for another two million dollars for year two, December, 2003 to December, 2004.

After the trip to Boston, Danny and Louis drive back to New York City. They spend the New Year's 2004 holiday, with the same young women that they had Christmas and New Years with in 2002.

Daniel's girl is Italian. Her name is Jean. Jean is twenty-nine years old. She is tall, dark complexion, black hair and brown eyes. She is an immigration lawyer. Jean works in the Empire

State building. Her office is down the hall from Susan's law office. Jean graduated Fordham Law School, as did Susan. They are friends.

Louis girl is named Karin. She is twenty-seven years old. Karin is half Irish and half Brazilian. She is tall, light brown hair and blue eyes. Karin has an MBA degree from New York University and works on Wall Street. She is a pharmaceutical industry analyst.

I think these two guys and girls will be getting married one of these years.

The date is January 5, 2004. Louis and Danny have just departed New Jersey. They are flying from McGuire Air Force Base to Fort Bragg, North Carolina. They will remain at Fort Bragg for thirty days. They are now first lieutenants. They have been in the army for more than two years. Their initial service commitment was for three years. They have signed for another three years hitch. After the month at Fort Bragg, Danny and Louis are going to return to Monterrey, California for more language training. For the first ten weeks, Louis will get advanced training in the Persian Language. Danny will study advanced Arabic for the same ten weeks. After a few days leave, they will go back to school. Danny will learn basic Persian and Louis will study basic Arabic.

On Tuesday, the second of February, 2004, I receive an email from Seghar. It concerns the company Molay Biotech Incorporated.

Seghar writes, "We are researching and developing antidotes to the toxins of sporulating bacteria, such as anthrax. We are attempting to develop vaccines for a variety of different influenza causing viruses. Since we are not allowed to do certain types of stem cell research in the United States, Molay Biotech will bring in a partner from the United Kingdom. It is a private company that does stem cell research. The name is Roslyn Genetics Limited of London."

Three days later Friday, February 5, 2004, I receive the 2003 financial statements for Molay, Biotech. The US government paid the company two million dollars. One and a half million goes directly for the operating expenses of the company. The

James Cage

break down is: $250,000 general operating expenses, such as heat, electricity, office expenses, office employee salaries, legal and accounting fees, and state S Corporation Taxes. There are no Federal Taxes because the company has not generated any profits. The other $1,250,000 goes into research and development. This includes the salaries of the bioengineers involved in the project.

The $500,000 left over is distributed in the following manner. The breakdown is as follows: $100,000 Scotty, $100,000 Seghar, $100,000 Mario, $45,000 Daniel, $45,000 Louis and I receive $10,000. The company Molay Biotech Incorporated will retain $100,000. The distribution is one dollar per share to all the original shareholders of the company. All the shareholders, including me, will have to pay individual federal income tax. Scotty, Seghar, and Mario actively work in the company. During the past year, Seghar sent me some data. I did statistical analysis for the firm Molay Biotech. Therefore I will also be an active participant in the company. The distribution for us is taxed as earned income. Since Louis and Danny are in the service of the United States government, they are non-active participants in the company. Their distribution is capital gains. The documents also include a forward statement for the year 2004.

The forward statement reads, "Roslyn Genetics LTD of London will invest $250,000 for a twenty percent share of the company." "Roslyn Genetics LTD receives 100,000 shares at $1.00 par value." "Therefore there are now 500,000 shares distributed and outstanding in Molay Biotech Inc. My 10,000 shares are now two percent of the company.

Daniel and Louis have done well this year financially. Their large apartments lease at $4000 per month. That brings in $96,000. They received $90,000 from Molay Biotech, which is their $100,000 investment back less the $10,000 I received. They earned another $125,000 from the Silicon Valley Software Company on the percentage of the software program sales. That equals $311,000 for the L&J Living Trust Fund. They made even more money from interest earned on their US Treasury Notes and the salary the army paid them.

The L&J Living Trust Fund pays me $1000 per month as accountant and executor. Susan as attorney and executor receives the same $1000 each month.

On Monday, the ninth of February, I visit Susan's law office to take care of business. When we are done with the affairs of the L&J Trust, I have Susan help me with personal legal documents. Susan drafts a will for me. The will includes the house in New Jersey, a bank account and brokerage account. The assets total $750,000. My cousin Nicky is the beneficiary of the will.

However, I have $1,500,000 in an overseas account. I had the name L&J Living Trust Fund added to the account. This way Danny and Louis automatically have the money in case anything happens to me. A will for this money is not necessary. Therefore all my assets are evenly divided between my cousin Nicky, Danny, and Louis. I tell Susan not to say anything to them until after I am dead.

On June 30, 2004 Danny and Louis go overseas. They are to be based in Qatar. After completion of the language classes in California, they returned to North Carolina. Then after thirty days they departed for Qatar.

Back In Time

By the end of July, 2004, the nightmares return and I cannot sleep. My mind goes back to 1996.

On Monday, May 20, 1996 I receive an email in my CompuServe account. It is from the Welshman. His name is Alan Sinclair, who I met in Guatemala many years ago. He sends me a telephone number. I know from the area code, it is a California number. I phone.

Alan Sinclair says, "Listen to the guy on this tape. Do you recognize the voice?"

Even though it has been fifteen years, I say, "Yes I know the voice."

He says, "I will mail you a set of instructions."

I answer, "OK."

On Sunday, the twenty-sixth of May I get into my tan, 1995 Toyota Corolla, leave New Jersey and drive to Knoxville,

Tennessee. The next day, Memorial Day, I drive through Nashville and Memphis to Conway, Arkansas. I have to stop because there are tornadoes in the area. Tuesday, I drive through the Ozark Mountains. The Ozarks are very pretty. There are wineries in this region of Arkansas. I rest in Fort Smith and drink a cup of coffee at McDonald's. I continue the journey on Interstate 40. I pass Indian Reservations in Oklahoma. I get caught in some traffic in Oklahoma City, drive through Amarillo, Texas and stop in Santa Rosa, New Mexico.

Wednesday morning I drive around the steep, curving, highway through Albuquerque. I pass the continental divide through Gallup and stop to eat a hamburger in Winslow, Arizona. I continue through mountains by Flagstaff and drive down to Kingman in the Mohave Desert. After a break, I head up Highway 93, drive over the Hoover Dam and finally arrive at Caesar's Palace in Las Vegas. I am registered for a five nights stay in the hotel.

Thursday Morning, May 30, 1996, I take a taxi to Fremont Street in downtown Las Vegas. I walk to the Greyhound Bus terminal and pay cash for an express bus ticket to Los Angeles. I have a false driver's license in case the ticket agent asks for identification. She does ask. I carry a sports bag and backpack. I am wearing a Dodger's baseball cap and sunglasses.

Early Thursday evening, Alan Sinclair picks me up at the bus station in Los Angeles. He is driving a blue Ford van. The printing on the side says Manny's Motor Parts. We drive to Marina Del Rey. We board a fair sized yacht. I say the length is seventy-five feet. Alan's brother Paolo (Paul) is driving the boat. Marcos diRandi is also aboard. These are the guys I met, twenty-five years ago at the Sambalanga Ranch in Guatemala. Marcos and Paul are medium height and build, thin, dark hair and eyes, tanned skin. Marco's age is early forties. The ages of Alan and Paul are middle forties. Paul is the younger brother. He is a physician and surgeon at a Kaiser Healthcare Center.

After going out to sea for twenty minutes, we enter the galley of the yacht. Alan unzips two body bags. Inside are two clothed, dead, Caucasian men. The men are each six feet tall. I check the bodies. There are no bullet holes on either body.

"I don't see any bullet holes?" I ask.

Marcos says, "We shot them with a dart gun. We hit them both in the neck." He shows me the small mark, near the right jugular vein on the neck of each victim."

Alan says, "The dart injects a poison made from: rattlesnake venom, lidocaine and a sedative hypnotic drug. When a victim is shot, he freezes for a second, stumbles another second or two, falls down and dies."

Then he says, "This is the body of the Surgeon. He is a real general surgeon. We got him last night walking from his office to his car in Huntington Beach."

I say, "Then this body is the Interrogator."

Alan says, "He is a former soldier. We got him in the parking lot of a diner, near the port in Long Beach."

Marcos says, "He had just eaten breakfast. It was early this morning and still dark outside when we hit him."

I ask, "Did you do anything with their cars?"

"No," Alan says. He continues, "The Surgeon's car is in his office parking lot and the Interrogator's car is parked in the diner's lot. In a few days, someone will report these guys missing. The police will find the cars. There is no evidence of foul play. Both men disappeared."

I say, "I bet these guys have disappeared a number of times."

Marcos chimes in, "Yeah but this time it is a permanent disappearance for the both of them."

Everybody laughs.

Alan, explains some more. "Twenty plus years ago, the Interrogator and the Surgeon were involved in a heroin drug smuggling cartel. The stuff came mostly from Afghanistan. It was processed in Italy and France and distributed throughout Europe. Some stuff was shipped through Rotterdam to the ports in New York and New Jersey."

Paul then says, "The Surgeon went to medical school in Bologna, Italy. Obviously, he got involved in the drug business to make money to help pay his expenses for school. The Interrogator was always involved in this business, as far as we know."

Alan completes the story, "Ten years ago, a new drug cartel was formed. During this period, the Interrogator has been importing both cocaine and heroin from Latin America. The Surgeon stayed involved, in the drug business as an investor. His skills as a doctor were also utilized when required."

I answer, "I am not really sure if these guys grabbed me in Venice fifteen years ago. However, I will take your word for it because the voice on the tape that you played for me was the voice of the Interrogator in Venice."

The boat engine has stopped. We are floating on the ocean. Paul is on the deck with a fishing pole. Alan, Marcos and I are below deck, working on the corpses. We remove all clothing, undergarments, shoes and socks. We cut all labels from the garments. We place all the clothes in one bag. The clothes will be burned in an incinerator on shore.

Next, with a small axe, I chop off the hands and feet of both bodies. Alan uses a heavy saw and severs the heads of the dead guys. We place each separate head on a workbench. Marco's manages to pull out the teeth with pliers and a screwdriver. He puts all the teeth in a cup. He goes top deck and throws the cup full of teeth overboard. Meanwhile, Alan places all hands and feet of both victims in one heavy duty plastic bag with a ten pounds weight.

Now, Marcos, using the heavy saw and small axe cuts the arms and legs off of the Surgeon's torso. He places the arms and legs into four plastic bags and adds a five pounds weight to each bag. He does the exact same thing with the Interrogator's arms and legs.

Alan punctures the lobes of the lungs of each dead man's torso. He places each torso, into the two original, individual body bags that were brought on board the yacht. He adds five pounds of weight to each bag.

I say, "Is it really necessary to puncture the lungs?"

Alan says, "Even though I add the weights, puncturing the lungs makes certain the torsos will not float to the top. All these bags will be ripped open by sharks. The body parts will be eaten within a few hours."

Marcos and I do the best we can to collect all the bloody, fatty tissue that encrust the plastic sheets that cover the room. We cut up the plastic sheets and place them with weights into two bags.

Alan and Paul go into the captain's cabin. Paul drives the boat out to sea. For the next hour we throw the body part bags all over the Pacific Ocean. When we return to the marina it is 9 PM and it is completely dark.

Alan and I get into the Ford van and leave. Marcos and Paul remain to wash down the boat.

Alan stops off at the location of Manny's Motor Parts.

I ask Alan, "Who is Manny?"

Alan answers, "I'm Manny."

I say, "Nice place, Manny."

Alan laughs.

We leave the van at the work site. We get into Alan's car. He drives to a condominium in Newport Beach. We are too tired to go out for dinner.

The next morning we have breakfast at Denny's.

I say, "Are you driving me back to Vegas this morning?"

"Yes," Alan answers. Then he says, "Do you like my car."

Alan Sinclair has a brand new 1996 Bentley Azure. He tells me the color is Ming Blue.

I answer, "Yeah, this is some fancy machine."

He says, "We will be in Vegas in no time at all."

We take Highway 15 into Barstow and stop for a break.

I ask him, "Where are your brother and Marcos? Are they meeting us in Vegas?"

"No," answers Alan. "They stayed at the Holiday Inn in Redondo Beach last night. Paul will drive Marcos back to Phoenix this morning. Just to be careful, the four of us should not be seen together."

I ask, "What kind of car is Paul driving?"

He says, "A 1995 black, Cadillac STS."

I think, "These guys like cars."

During the ride to Las Vegas, Alan says, "Do you know why those guys grabbed you in Venice, years ago?"

I answer, "I figure, they had me confused with someone else."

He tells me, "That narcotics cartel had fairly good intelligence. They received word that a hit man was coming in to exterminate one of the leaders of their group. They thought you were the hit guy."

I say, "I thought maybe I was being used as a decoy. Did the package I gave you have any value to it?"

Alan answers, "You were not a decoy. I was the hit man. The document you gave me was the hit list. It contained the names and places of targets located throughout Europe. They got you and missed me."

Then I ask, "Were the targets hit?"

Alan says, "All those targets were hit within the year."

I sing, "That's all over now."

Alan and I have a good time in Vegas. We gamble a little and meet a couple of women from Seattle, Washington. One afternoon, Marcos calls the hotel. He asks me if I would you be interested in visiting him in Phoenix.

I answer, "Sure."

On Monday, the third of June, Alan decides to stay at Caesar's another day. I pack my car. It has been safely parked at Caesar's the last few days. I drive south on Highway 93, all the way to Phoenix. It is a slow, hot ride. When I arrive in Phoenix I stop at a motel near the airport. When I am settled in, I give Marcos a call.

We have a steak dinner and beer in a fine restaurant across the street from the motel.

Marcos asks, "Do you do cleaning jobs often?"

"No," I answer. "I never was a cleaner. The last time I did a cleaning job was so long ago, I cannot remember."

Marcos says, "That hit was my last job, I am retiring. I'm going down to Mexico for a while. Then I may settle in Costa Rica."

"That sounds good to me."

He says, "How have you been doing."

I answer, "Ok, The Controller has me pick up and deliver packages. Every week, I pick something up in Manhattan and deliver it to Midtown or Downtown. I keep an apartment in New York City. I meet the Controller there sometimes. I also bring documents to Philadelphia, Atlantic City and Washington DC. I drive from my New Jersey house to make those deliveries. The jobs are easy and not dangerous. I make a lot of money. I don't make as much money as you and Alan do shooting targets. But, I make enough."

Marcos says, "Do you meet the Controller in your apartment?"

"Yes, but not all the time. Sometimes I meet him in a restaurant or Central Park."

Then he asks, "What do you do with all your spare time?"

I answer, "I take college courses, one or two classes each semester. I may be getting a regular job in September to fill up the time. I am tired of going to school. The students are getting younger and I am getting older."

"What kind of work will you be doing?"

"Accounting work for a firm in Newark, New Jersey," I answer.

On Tuesday, the fourth of June, I drive on Highway 10 from Phoenix, to Tuscan then over to El Paso, Texas. I enjoy riding near the Mexican border. I stay on Highway 10 and cut north on Interstate 20. I stop for the evening in Pecos, Texas. I like the big sky and rolling hills of southwest Texas.

On Wednesday, I drive past the oil wells in Odessa and Midland. I continue the ride through Abilene and stop for a coffee break at a McDonald's in Fort Worth. I drive through Dallas and the highway changes to Interstate 30. Texarkana is where I stop and spend the night.

Thursday, the ride continues. I pass through the small town of Hope, Arkansas, the home of the President of the United States. Then I drive through Little Rock and the highway becomes Interstate 40. I chug across the Memphis Bridge and drive through Nashville, going all the way to Knoxville, Tennessee.

On Friday, June 7, 1996, I am back home in New Jersey. I enjoyed the ride through Texas immensely.

Back to Present

On August 14, 2004, Danny emails me from Iraq. Now he is a qualified translator and interrogator for the army. I hope he does his job properly. It is not necessary to torture prisoners. There are always informants. It is easiest to pay the informant money and get information. A true believer is not going to talk even under torture.

Danny writes from Baghdad, "I am back in the Green Zone in Baghdad. Some of the marines and soldiers have been complaining about the siege of Fallujah, this past April, 2004. They were forced by the political authorities to pull out. The military people here say we are going to have to go back into Fallujah and clean out the city."

Danny continues, "Because the insurgents are killing many Iraqi civilians, we are beginning to get more cooperation and better information from Iraqis. Too many terrorists are coming across the border from Syria and Iran. There are not enough military personnel to control the borders."

I write, "I am glad the government is training American soldiers, like you, to speak and understand Arabic." It is not possible to fully trust a non-American translator."

I add, "There are not enough soldiers to control the border between the United States and Mexico. To lock down the borders of Iraq is impossible."

In September, 2004, Louis sends an email.

"Greetings from Kabul, I am learning more about the Muslim religion. There are one billion Muslims in the world; ninety percent are Sunni Muslims. In Afghanistan eighty percent of the population is Sunni Muslim. However in Iran to the west the population is eighty-nine percent, Shia Muslim. The difference is the Sunnis worship the first four Caliphs as Muhammad's successors. The Shiites recognize only the fourth, Ali as the spiritual head of state. The spread of the Islamic revolution comes from Saudi Arabia. The Saudi's are Sunni Muslims. They follow a strict form of the religion named Wahhabism. The Saudi's have funded Wahhabi oriented religious schools throughout the world. These religious schools are even in the USA."

Louis continues, "The Taliban is in the south. They are in Baluchistan Territory that crosses southwest Pakistan into Iran. Osama is supposed to be hiding out in the northeastern mountains between Afghanistan and Pakistan. Special Forces soldiers patrol that area. They come across some hardened, well, trained enemy combatants. Our soldiers have not found Osama or his lieutenants."

I email back and write, "Osama is probably living in a decent home in Islamabad, Pakistan. No one in Pakistan is going to give up their hero."

Louis answers, "When I have leave, the first week in November, Danny and I will be together in London. We are meeting with the financier of Roslyn Genetics. Seghar, Scotty and Mario will also be at the meeting. You are welcome to come to the meeting. The L&J Trust will pay all your expenses."

I email again, "I don't like to fly so I won't be going to London. But I hope all you guys, have a good time when you visit blimey, old England."

It is Saturday, November 13, 2004 (Eid) Al FITR, the end of the holy month of Ramadan. This day on the Muslim Calendar is the Festival of Sacrifice. Louis, Danny, Seghar, Scotty and Mario have just met the owner and chairman of Roslyn Genetics in jolly, old London.

Danny's email reads, "The name of the chairman of Roslyn Genetics is Lord G.F. Richmond. He is a large man, not heavy. He is at least six feet four inches tall. He has thick, white hair. He appears to be in his early seventies. His skin is fair and unwrinkled. "He has a pleasant smile and looks like an actor. All of us are very impressed with him. Because we were all educated at MIT, he is interested in us. He has a specific curiosity for synthetic biology. He says with our computer, engineering skills and knowledge of biology we should be able to genetically manipulate bacteria to behave like machines.

Lord Richmond said this has been researched at Universities in Texas and California."

Danny's email continues, "When we return to the states, Louis and I have to report directly to Fort Bragg, North Carolina. Then we go to Monterrey, California. Karin and Jean will join us in California for Christmas. You are always welcome."

My email reads, "I am glad your meeting went well with Lord Richmond. I will spend Christmas with my cousin's family in New Jersey. I will catch you guys on your return back east."

I immediately do an Internet Search on Lord G.F. Richmond. Lord Richmond was born on December 21, 1916 in Paris, France. That would make him almost eighty-eight years old, not early seventies. His father was a Russia aristocrat attached to the embassy in Paris. His mother was an English Lady and distant cousin to the King. He was educated, as a boy, by private tutors. Later in his youth, he attended Oxford. At the age of twenty-one Richmond enlisted in the British Military. During World War II he served as an officer in the British Special Forces.

I find his biography to be very sketchy. There is no picture of him. There is no mention of his military unit or rank. It gives a listing of corporations, banks and charities he has been associated with during his business career. He does not have a wife or children.

It is Wednesday, February 9, 2005. It is both Ash Wednesday and Chinese New Year. Louis sends me an email from Washington, DC.

Louis says, "Danny and I are going to be attached to the Pentagon. We are going to return to the Middle East in a few days, probably Qatar. We will be together. Our tour will be four months. We have both received the rank of Captain."

Louis continues, "Lord Richmond has invested another two million dollars for research in Molay Biotech Inc. Mario has been designing complicated biological circuitry. These Biobricks, strings of DNA, are programmed bacteria. The programmed bacteria may lay dormant in a cell. If the cell becomes cancerous, the programmed bacteria, turns on and stops the cancer. Seghar and Scotty are developing vaccines. They have developed one vaccine that is specific for the bird flu virus that is starting to spread from Asia. They have to find a quick and inexpensive method to manufacture the vaccine. The money from Lord Richmond will benefit this research tremendously. We would like you to be a part of this research. Would you be interested in doing a statistical analysis for us?"

I email, "Sure, whenever you want, I will do the analysis. Have a safe trip."

In early May, 2005, I receive an email from Seghar.

He writes, "Lord Richmond will be at a meeting in Washington, DC from Tuesday, the eighteenth of May through Saturday, the twenty-second of May. He has some documents that he wants to hand deliver. He will be unable to come up to Boston. Scotty and I are in the middle of research work. Would it be possible for you to pick up the documents on Friday, the twentieth of May? He will be at the L'Enfant Hotel. Are you familiar with the hotel and Washington, DC?"

I write, "I will be there."

On Friday, May 20, 2005 I take the Acela Express train from Metro Park in New Jersey. I reach the hotel at 3:00 PM. At 5:00 PM, I call the room of Lord Richmond.

He answers, "Hello."

I say, "I'll meet you downstairs in ten minutes if that is OK with you?"

He says, "See you."

When I see Lord George Foster Richmond he walks up to me and shakes my hand. He looks good for eighty-nine years old."

I say, "Do the boys know that we know each other and that I worked for you my entire adult life?"

The Bear answers, "How could they possibly know?"

Then he says, "Do Danny and Louis know who you are?"

"Yes, I am pretty sure they know who I am."

The Bear asks, "Tell me about their mothers."

I say, "I knew their mothers. In January, 1973, I was a permanent substitute teacher in a high school in New Jersey. In the evenings, I took some psych classes in Jersey City. I enrolled in an abnormal psychology class on a Monday and

Wednesday nights. I also had a social psychology class on Tuesday and Thursday nights."

I continue. "Danny's mother was in my abnormal psych class. Her name was Valerie. She was a senior and graduating from the college in Jersey City in June. "Valerie was a premed student and was going to start medical school in September. She was to be married upon graduation from college. She told me that she was not sure she wanted to be married."

I say, "Louis's mother's name was Rita. She was in the social psych class. She was graduating City College in Manhattan at the end of the semester. She picked up this extra psychology class in Jersey City. She told me it was easy to take the Path Train from New York City to Journal Square in Jersey City and take the bus down Kennedy Blvd to school. Rita told me she was pretty sure she was getting a job, teaching elementary school in Manhattan in September, 1973. She told me her boyfriend was in the army and wanted to be married before leaving for Vietnam. She was not sure she wanted to marry him."

I speak some more, "The early seventies was sex, drugs and rock and roll. A glass of wine, a joint and a half Quaalude and things happen. By the way, the girls did not know each other."

The Bear asks, "Did you ever see them again?"

I answer, "I went back to Mexico in the summer of 1973 and did not see either of them for many years. I met Valerie at a New York Hospital in the spring of 1980. I was with my cousin Nicky. He was having an interview for an externship at the hospital. Valerie told me that she was in her second year of residency. She started medical school one year later because she had a baby. She said her husband had died. She asked me how I was. I said fine. That was the conversation."

I continue, "I ran into Rita a few weeks later in a nightclub on Forty Ninth Street. She was with a boyfriend. She told me she was teaching grade school over at York Avenue and Seventy-Eighth Street."

The Bear says, "Isn't that where you had the apartment?"

"Yes." "When I got the apartment on Seventy-Eighth Street, I went into the school and asked if Rita was teaching there. The office told me she was teaching at another school on the Upper East Side."

I continue to talk, "Rita told me her husband was killed in Vietnam. She said she had a six and a half year old son named Louis. Rita introduced me to her new boyfriend but I don't recall his name. That was the last time I saw her."

I say, "In early 1997, I would see Danny and Louis running together in Central Park. Occasionally I'd see them on the subway. When I went for an interview at L&J Incorporated they knew me. I thought they might be brothers or cousins when I met them. After time passed, they told me about their mothers. When Danny and Louis met at MIT, they must have noticed the resemblance to one another. I suspect their mothers told them something at that time."

The Bear says, "Then by random chance, in 1998, you walk into their office for a job?"

I answer, "Yes, just random probability."

He says, "Do you really believe that?"

I answer, "I had a couple of acquaintances that I would see during races in Central Park. I mentioned that I was looking for an accounting position. One young woman pointed to Danny and Louis after a four miles race. "She told me the name of L&J Incorporated and that there was an advertisement for an accounting job in the newspaper." She wanted to introduce me to them on the spot. I said. 'Don't bother the guys. I will check out the ad. If I am qualified, I'll apply for the job.' I guess that is not exactly random probability."

The Bear says. "I always paid you a lot of money. You did not need a job."

I say, "I needed to keep busy. "I did not like waiting around thinking."

The Bear and I walk from the L'Enfant Hotel to the Washington Memorial.

He says, "What a shame. Such great men such as Washington, Franklin and Jefferson founded the United States. Now you have a government controlled by money from Arab oil sheiks and lobbyists. The politicians are a greedy lot."

I say, "Look at the leadership in Europe. They were all on the take from Sadaam. With the exception of Great Britain, the USA doesn't have any powerful allies in Europe."

Then I ask, "What will the future bring?"

The Bear says, "The Middle East will explode. It may take a few more years. The mullahs in Iran are getting ready for an apocalyptic battle. They just about have a nuclear bomb."

I say, "If I were Iran, I would definitely want a nuclear bomb. Pakistan, India and Israel all have nukes. It is natural for a country to want to protect its people."

The Bear continues, "When Iran gets a nuke, Israel and the US will have to blow up the facilities. The Muslim world will explode. There will be an uprising all over the Middle East, Indonesia, Europe and even the United States. An entire division of terrorists may have crossed the Mexican border into this country over the past ten years. There will be trouble in the cities of the United States."

I say, "I read a book that say's the Oklahoma City bombing was an Iraqi intelligence operation. They found a disgruntled American and used him."

He says, "That sounds true. The bomb was the same type that blew up the Kohbar Towers in Saudi Arabia, on June 25, 1996. Also, Iraqi intelligence helped finance the first World Trade Center bombing in 1993."

I am thinking, "To paraphrase a song from the movie, *Chicago*," I say, "Then Iraq, had it coming."

The Bear laughs and says, "But of course."

After some time we reach the Lincoln Memorial.

The Bear says, "What a pity that this country had slavery."

I say, "That should never have happened. However, presently, aren't most people economic slaves?"

He says, "Most people are robots. They are part of a great machine."

I say, "I've always felt like a robot, a genetically programmed killer. You put a gun in my hand and I pull the trigger. It is a reflex action to me. It always has been."

The Bear says, "You did not kill at random. Your targets were the really bad guys. He continues to speak, "Do you have any remorse about the things you have done."

I answer, "You are the Controller. You gave me the targets. I have no remorse about the killings. I was doing my job. That's it. As far as my normal life goes, I always minded my own business, did not bother anyone and kept my mouth shut."

He says, "You killed a few people on your own."

"Yeah, but they had it coming." I laugh.

We continue our walk toward the Vietnam Memorial. I say, "There are 50,000 names here. What did they die for?"

He says, "Soldiers die in war. In past history, a war was fought to win. Genghis Khan or Attila the Hun killed the enemy and conquered the land. World War II was fought to win. Korea, Vietnam and Iraq are wars of containment. A war of containment cannot be won. Over time if Iraq survives, it will be split three ways. The Kurds will control the north, the Sunnis the central area and the Shiites the southern part of Iraq."

Even though it is early evening, it is still light out. The Bear hails a taxi and we go to a seafood restaurant. We both order salmon fillets, rice, and salad and Merlot wine.

At dinner I ask again, "What will happen in the future? The world is falling apart."

He says, "Russia and China can line up with Iran against the USA and Europe. If that happens, we get an all-out nuclear war."

He continues, "If I were you, I would not live on the east coast or the west coast. I would move to the Rocky Mountains."

I answer, "I may do that." I change the subject and ask, "What about the documents you have for me."

He explains, "I will give you the documents when we return to the hotel. Those young guys have a great deal of talent. When they have the vaccines fully developed, I am going to make sure that the vaccinations will be available to the public. I have a company in Canada that will manufacture and distribute any vaccines Molay Biotech Inc. produces. I will keep this out of the hands of the major pharmaceutical companies. Those companies will delay the process. The documents contain information about the cost structure for the manufacturing and distribution of the vaccine."

I ask, "Have you done anything to help Louis and Danny."

He says, "I gave their names to someone in the Department of Defense. They will become permanent intelligence analysts at the Pentagon. They are completely qualified and have served their government well. They are more valuable serving the United States here in DC, than being in the field."

"Good," I say.

The Bear says, "Be careful the watchers are watching us."

I say, "You're a controller and you worry about the watchers?"

He says, "It is the evil watchers that concern me. Do you know the difference?"

I answer, "Yes. Years ago, I had recurring dreams. In one specific dream, I would be driving around the city of Guadalajara, Mexico in a taxicab. A Mexican cab driver, who wore a cowboy hat, would pull the taxi over and tell me. 'I am Saint Michael the Archangel. I have had a very difficult time watching you and keeping you alive. Start taking better care of yourself.' "

I explain some more. "The Mexican cab driver is a good watcher. He protected me."

The Bear says, "What about the bad watchers?"

I say, "When I see them, I walk the other way."

He says, "Have you had any upsetting dreams lately."

I answer, "I don't have too many dreams. The hell dreams have subsided. I die. I go into the Bardo. The demons continually attack me. They stab, cut and beat me. They gouge out my eyes. In the dream, I wake up. Then the demons attack and kill me again."

"Explain any other dreams," he asks.

"I have absence of God dreams. I am in a cold, gray place. I am alone. Some souls flick on through. Once in a while, someone I know, who has died passes. They never speak or acknowledge my existence. This place is not evil but there is absence of light."

I continue, "Another place in hell, are the night scene dreams. These dreams take place in a nightclub. There is hard, heavy, metal music. The sound is a continuing drone. The people here are really evil. When I walk through the place, these souls do not speak to me. They telepathically let me know, I do not belong here, get out. I add, "Some casinos in Las Vegas and Atlantic City have a similar feel to it."

Then I say, "I have never gone to heaven, so I cannot describe that."

When we return to the hotel, The Bear goes over the documents with me.

I ask, "Maybe I should FedEx these papers tomorrow morning, directly to Seghar. They should be safe."

The Bear says, "Do that."

Late Saturday afternoon, May 21, 2005, I exit the Amtrak train at Metro Park, New Jersey. I am approaching my car in the enclosed, parking lot. The unmarked, white van pulls in front me. That is the last thing I ever see alive. My head bursts open. I wasn't watching the watchers and they got me.

The Bardo

I am in the Bardo now. The hell beasts and demons are attacking me. But it is different than in my dreams. This time, I beat the hell out of them. I gouge out their eyes and kill them all. When it starts all over again, I kill them all again.

After a time, I am out of the Bardo. It is judgment time for me. Azrael and Malik are reviewing my life. They give me a choice. I can relive my life again. I can have a full lifetime. I can have a job, wife and children. The only catch is I have to live and die in New Jersey.

I ask, Azrael, "What is the other alternative?"

Azrael says, "You have to spend a few eons in hell to pay for your sins."

I answer, "I'll do the time in hell. I've already lived in New Jersey."

Azrael says, "Then go with Malik."

Malik tells me, "Not to worry. You are not going to the lowest depths of hell with the politicians and corrupt corporate executives, the evil controllers and watchers. You will be with souls as you are."

I am in hell now. The Fire-Eater in the middle of the road, smiles at me. In the distance I can hear the hard rock, bar music. But I am not going over there.

I sit at a table. I see two guys that I knew when I was a teenager. They died at seventeen years old. I am not sure if they were killed in accidents or by suicide. They look thirty-five years old. Everyone looks thirty-five years old. Someone taps me on the shoulder. I turn around and it is Pancho Villa. I rode with him in another life.

He says, "Bienvenido Jaime. Long time no see."

I say, "Good to see you again, Pancho."

Pancho sits down next to me. Then Pancho says, "Do you have any regrets from your past life?"

I answer, "I would have liked to have spent more time in Paris. Also, I wanted to live until December, 2012. According to the Mayan Calendar, that is the end of an age. I did not make it."

Pancho says, "You are better off in hell with me."
"Yes," I say, "This is where I belong."
A waitress comes by and brings us food.
Pancho says, "Eat the food. It's good."
Some other souls come to the table, sit and eat.
Yes, we all have lunch together.

James Cage

Cover Design
The Cowboy
By Alan Mahood
Copyright © 2012 Alan Mahood
C-ART Gallery
Newport Beach, CA

Book IV: The Mind of Frank Rosseus

The Assignment Friday, May 11

I enter the elevator and press the button. The door closes. As the lift rises, background music plays softly. The sound is Texas Rockabilly. In the seven years I've been in this place I have never gone above the fourth level. I am going uptown and exit the elevator at the ninety-ninth floor.

It is drab and dusty within the lower levels but the top level is very bright and clean. The light bothers me. With trepidation, I walk toward the large door at the end of the hallway and question, "Why have I been summoned?"

As I am about to knock on the greenish, blue door, it opens and I pass through.

At the large table in the center of the meeting hall, two beings sit in comfortable chairs. Sunlight dashes through the shades. I stop and stand uncomfortably before them in the middle of the room. This is the first time I face The Chairman. On his right side, The Chairman's second in command sits. He is known as The Cowboy. The Cowboy removes his hat and rises from his seat.

The Cowboy opens a book and speaks, "Jaime, you've been with us now for seven years. You are punctual, follow orders and have made significant progress. Your clean record and previous experience qualify you for this position. You will replace someone who is unable to continue his life cycle.

The shades close. A vision, similar to a movie video on a screen displays on the far wall. A man about forty years old, my height and build quickly walks across a street. He appears to be very fit and in the prime of life. Suddenly he is hit by a yellow taxi cab. After a sequence of scenes, the young man is spread out on an operating table in a hospital amphitheater.

The Cowboy says, "Jaime, you will become this man. However, you will retain your own mind."

The Chairman speaks, "You can option out."

The Cowboy adds, "You will not be alone on this assignment. You will have help from others and I will be in constant contact watching you."

I know I must answer in the affirmative. I have no choice in the matter. I will be thrust into the constant battle between good and evil in the heavens and on earth.

"I will take the assignment sir," I answer.

In the fraction of a second that I accept the assignment, I awaken in a critical care recovery room. The doctors are removing tubes from my nose and throat. I am a living body. Everything hurts and my throat is very dry. I can sense the physicians are thrilled with the patient's miraculous recovery from head trauma. My body is banged up but there are no broken bones. When the physicians leave the room, I look at the plastic bracelet on my left wrist. I am in Beth Israel Hospital, New York City. The date of admittance is May 11, 2012. My name is Frank Rosseus.

From Frank's memory bank, I absorb his history. Frank was born on November 10, 1973 in New York City. Frank was adopted at four days old. At the time of the adoption his parents were middle aged. He was their only child. His father was a corporate lawyer and his mother was an accountant. Frank went to private schools in New York City. He graduated NYU with two degrees, a BS in Finance and MBA. Both parents died from natural causes a few years ago. They were in their mid-eighties when they passed. Frank never cared to know anything about his natural parents. He loved the mother and father that adopted him.

Frank is a rich young man with all the finer things in life. He is a general partner with the stock and options trading company Burke Partners located on lower Broadway. Presently, his net worth is over twenty-four million dollars. This does not include the Sutton Place apartment he inherited. Now that I know something about Frank's detailed skills, abilities, history and memories, I hope to be able to recall these memories as needed. My mind understands the fundamental knowledge contained inside Frank's brain matter. However Frank's soul, his spirit, his essence of being has moved on. My soul, spirit and mind have transmigrated completely into the body and brain of Frank Rosseus.

The best explanation for the spirit is this quote from *The Yajur Veda.* *"The inspired Self is not born nor does He die. He springs from nothing and becomes nothing; unborn, permanent, unchanging, primordial. He is not destroyed when the body is destroyed."*

This Hindu explanation of the Self is in direct contrast to the electro-biochemical reactions that take place in the human brain. Neuroscientists' describe the physiology and anatomy of the brain as the Mind. This means when the brain dies, you die.

Frank's soul and spirit have moved to a higher level of existence. However his brain is not dead. His physical brain functions but my mind is inside controlling electro-biochemical synthesis.

It was beneficial for me to spend one week in the hospital becoming Frank. The time was necessary for psychic adjustment. The physical body had to be monitored. There were constant blood tests and brain scans. I had aches and pains, dizziness and headaches.

Office of Roslyn Genetics Limited London, England

Present at the meeting: Lord George Foster Richmond, Chairman of the Board of Roslyn Genetics. He sits at the head of the table. Five other men are also present. These men control media, industry, finance, politicians and the world in general. They plan wars, population surveillance, mind control and the destiny of the world. Their goal is to keep the human population under constant stress and fear. With the exception of Lord Richmond, these five men are demonic, satanic entities. Their goal is to destroy human spirituality. They are evil.

Friday, May 18

This morning is Friday, the eighteenth of May. The hospital calls my apartment. Lupe, my friend and caretaker, answers. Twenty-five minutes later she arrives at the hospital. I recognize her immediately. She stands in the foyer of the waiting room. I walk up to her. She gives me a hug and says, "*Cómo está Frankie.*"

"I am fine, Lupe."

Lupe has a taxi waiting. This is my first time outside the hospital. The apartments across from Beth Israel Hospital on First Avenue appear familiar to me. We get into the cab and drive uptown. I turn my head and take one more look at those apartments.

Lupe is a plump, middle aged woman. She is sixty-six years old. She was born in Aguascalientes, Mexico. Her family legally migrated to the United States in the 1950's. Her husband died many years ago. She has a son, who works for the federal government. He lives in El Paso, Texas. He has a wife and two small children, a boy and girl. Lupe also has a daughter who is a school teacher. She lives with her husband in Buffalo, New York. She has a five year old daughter. Lupe has worked for the Rosseus family for forty-five years. She helped bring Frank up. She owns a two bedroom apartment on the West Side. Lupe also has her own large bedroom and private bath at Frank's condominium on Sutton Place. Frank pays her salary of ninety-five thousand dollars per year plus supplemental health insurance to cover the medical bills that Medicare doesn't pay. Frank wants to give her a raise but Lupe says, "You pay me enough money. I don't work very hard anymore."

I sit in the spacious living room of Frank's, apartment and try to sort things out. I think this place is way too big. Frank has lived here his entire life. Lupe walks into the room and gives me a cup of herbal tea.

I inhale the fumes of the tea. "Lupe please take back the tea and bring me a cup of café con leche."

"You want café con leche?"

"Yes."

"You have not asked for that since you were a teenager."

I say, "Oh, I just have a desire for it."

She looks at me a bit strangely and says, "Coming right up."

I close my eyes and check Frank's memories. He has no relatives or family. Frank had two girlfriends. His first girl left him for someone else ten years ago. Three years ago, his last girlfriend, Linda, wanted to marry him but Frank wasn't ready. She married a prominent neurologist and they moved to Wilkes-Barre, Pennsylvania. Frank has been alone ever since. He is content to remain a bachelor. Frank does not smoke, drink or take drugs. Frank is not a womanizer. He is a workaholic and a moneymaker.

Memories of my past life have been suppressed. Although I have self-awareness, I don't remember exactly who I was. I don't know what type of work I did. I cannot remember parents or if I had any family, wife or children. My mind is befuddled because I can remember actors, books, television personalities and major events. My memories go back over sixty years. I remember President Eisenhower's speech to beware of the military industrial complex. I remember when John F. Kennedy, Martin Luther King and Bobby Kennedy were shot. I clearly remember Lee Harvey Oswald getting killed by Jack Ruby on television. Frank was born in 1973, so these are not his memories. Whatever I did in my past life, it could not have been good. I am paying for my sins with this assignment. I understand that over time my past life experiences will return.

I also have what I call, crackpot memories. I remember Leotis Martin knocking out Sonny Liston at the International Hotel in Las Vegas, Nevada in June, 1969. Why do I remember that? I must have been a boxing fan. I remember the USA landing on the moon July 20, 1969. Of course I watched the moon landing on television but where? Las Vegas, I don't think so. Perhaps I watched the moon landing in Los Angeles, California? Yeah that's it. I saw Apollo II land on the moon when I was in LA.

Inside my head music plays, and I sing softly, "I've been good, Dallas, Texas, Hollywood."

New York City Thursday, May 24

My controller is sending me psychic instructions. This is driving me crazy. I need to remove these signals from my head. A great aspect of human existence is that a human being can exert some control over his or hers own mind. I need to buy a book to learn how to control the mind of Frank Rosseus.

I walk from my apartment on Sutton Place west on Fifty-Sixth Street. I cross Fifth Avenue, proceed south and enter the Barnes and Noble Bookstore near Forty-Sixth Street. I purchase a book about meditation by K. McDonald. I'll study these meditation techniques and block the controller's messages.

I watch the patrons in the bookstore. Their expressions appear contorted. Some of the faces are melting. I snap back to reality and exit Barnes and Noble. I check my reflection in the window. I am nattily dressed in a Brooks Brothers' standard white shirt with the buttoned down collar, a fine tan sports jacket and expensive soft, malleable brown shoes. The reflection, in the window is me. I ask a young woman passing by to take my picture.

"Excuse me Miss. Can you take my picture? I am not sure how to use this smart phone."

The woman shows me how to use the smart phone. She clicks the photo.

When I view the picture, the face in the digital image is Frank Rosseus. We appear very similar at the age of thirty-eight years old. Frank and I look like brothers.

I tell the woman. "Thank you."

She smiles and walks away. She is very attractive from behind.

I walk up Fifth Avenue toward the park. I hurry across Central Park South into Central Park. The weather is warm. At noon I have a meeting with a New York City Police Detective at the boathouse inside the park.

I see the detective lieutenant standing directly in front of the boat house. You can't miss him. He is six feet tall, very lean with a fair complexion. He is about forty years old. He is four inches taller than I am. The detective's name is Louis Rodriguez with a G, not a Q and a Z not a S.

I did a search on NYPD's website for Louis Rodriguez. He is highly educated with an advanced degree from MIT. He served in the military for six years. He joined the New York City Police Department in 2007. I wonder how he became a detective lieutenant in only five years. I figure he must be assigned to a special division.

Detective Rodriguez spoke to me briefly at the hospital. He said the accident was a hit and run. Yesterday, I received a call from him. He wanted to meet with me. I suggested Central Park. Why did I suggest Central Park? Maybe I lived in the city before and enjoyed Central Park? Or did Frank like Central Park? Anyway I had gone to Frank's office, Monday, Tuesday and Wednesday and I wanted to go someplace else in the city on Thursday.

Today is an especially beautiful day. I walk up to Louis Rodriguez and we shake hands.

He says, "You look well Frank, how's the head?"

"My head feels strange. The sounds of the city are sometimes loud and at other times muffled. My hearing is not one hundred percent clear. When I listen to Maria Bartiroma on CNBC she sounds like Barbara Walters."

The detective laughs. We sit down at the Boathouse Restaurant and order coffee.

Louis says, "The accident you were involved in may have been attempted murder. The cab was stolen. We have two videos from security cameras on Canal Street showing that the taxi driver made no effort to brake or avoid hitting you. Can you recall the events of that evening?"

"On Friday night, the eleventh of May at 8:30 PM, I got off the number six subway train at the Canal Street Station. I was meeting my business partners for a late dinner at a Chinese restaurant on Mott Street. I was crossing Canal Street at the cross walk and don't remember anything after that."

"You are a principal partner in the stock trading firm Burke Partners, correct?"

"Yes, I was meeting John Burke, the president of the firm, Richard Stanley the chief financial officer and Alan Sinclair the head trader. We meet at a restaurant most Friday evenings to go over the week's trading events and set strategies for Monday morning."

Louis says, "You are vice-president of the company?"

'I am vice-president in charge of human resources. I also do trading and corporate strategy when necessary."

"What is the breakdown of the partnership?"

"John, Richard, Alan and I have equal shares in the company. We each own twenty percent. The associate partners Peter Murzenski and Keith Sprague split six percent of the firm's profits but they have no voting rights in the partnership. As the company expands we will add another associate partner. Then the three associates will split ten percent of the net profits. The last ten to fourteen percent is for employee bonuses, research and development and cash on hand."

"How many people work in the firm?"

"We are a small company. There are John, Richard, Alan, Peter, Keith and me. That makes six. Than we have three junior traders: Loren Holmes, Samuel Nunn and Lucille Ortega. Plus three administrative assistants: Janice DeMarco, Carolyn Murphy and Andrew Moreno. That makes twelve of us."

"Can you email me information on your personnel including each employee's address, telephone number and email?"

"I'll do that today, detective."

Detective Rodriguez hands me his card which includes his email address.

He says, 'I did not give you my card at the hospital because you were out of it. I felt you needed more time to recover from your head injuries."

Louis continues, "Tell me about the stock trading business."

"We trade stock and stock options. All trades are completed by the end of each day. There are never any trade carryovers for the next morning. Presently high frequency trading cartels control the daily trading business. My company does very well competing against them because we developed proprietary computer program strategies and algorithms. Some of our young traders are studying the bond, commodities and currency markets. We are running simulations on these markets but have not made any trades. In the future we shall trade the currency and commodities markets daily. Trading strategy is different for bonds. We may hold some international bonds for long term investment."

The detective asks, "Explain to me what these high frequency trading outfits do."

"This is a simple example. A high frequency trading company will buy one million shares of stock and break it down into lots of 500 or 1000 shares. They sell the shares when the stock increases by two cents. They make twenty thousand dollars in a few seconds. If they do that ten times in one hour with ten stocks they make two hundred thousand dollars. If they trade all day they can make a million dollars."

"Do the cartels ever lose?"

I answer, "Hardly ever, the trading cartels receive information before the general public and front run stocks. They have high speed computers located next to trading centers and complete trades fractions of seconds before slower trading groups. They trade fast and often. Occasionally someone makes an input error or there is a computer glitch. But things usually run smoothly."

"Isn't front running a stock against the rules?

"Yes, but the way the cartels trade, in fractions of a second, it would be impossible to prove front running,"

"So, how does Burke Partners compete against them?"

"Specifically, Dr. Alan Sinclair developed computer algorithms that track these high frequency trading systems. We follow some of their methodology. We also develop, improve and implement our own strategies."

Louis says, "No one outside of Burke uses your computer trading program?

"No, the program is proprietary for our company." Then I ask, "Detective, why is a highly educated man like you working for the NYPD and specifically on my case?"

Louis Rodriguez smiles and says, "Did you look me up on the Internet?"

"Yes, I checked you out detective."

Louis answers my question. "I work in a special division. That evening, Friday the eleventh of May, I was the supervisory detective at the downtown precinct. A patrol officer called in the hit and run. A detective has to investigate a hit and run accident. I need to tell you something Frank. Because Burke Partners are international traders, the federal government will be part of this investigation. FBI Special Agent Daniel Johnson is also assigned to this case. When is it convenient for you to see us?"

"We can meet Monday at my apartment. It's Memorial Day and my office is closed. How about noon time? My friend, Lupe, will make us lunch. The apartment is on Sutton Place."

"I have your address. We will be there at noon," answers Detective Louis Rodriguez.

When I get home, I remember that Detective Rodriguez requested a list of all Burke Partners employees. I retrieve two files from the folder Burke Partners. The first file includes a list of employees' names, ages, education and beginning date of employment at Burke. The second file contains the telephone numbers, street addresses and emails for all personnel. I email both files to Detective Rodriguez.

At 3:00 PM on Thursday, the twenty-fourth of May, Louis Rodriguez receives the Burke Partner files and forwards them to FBI Special Agent Daniel Johnson.

In the downtown office of the Federal Bureau of Investigation, a telephone rings. Special Agent Daniel Johnson answers, "Hello."

"Danny, did you get the files I just sent you?"

"I am looking at them now."

"Rosseus came up clean when you ran his FBI background check. Run a background report on everyone in the firm."

"Will do," says Danny.

"Can you meet me Monday at noon on the southwest corner of Sutton Place and East Fifty-Sixth Street?"

"I'll be there, Louis."

Doing Lunch Monday, May 28

Guadalupe enters the Rosseus apartment at 8 AM, Monday the twenty-eighth of May, Memorial Day morning. She hears sounds and smells food cooking in the kitchen.

"Frankie, what are you doing?"

"I am making sauce and meatballs for the two police officers that are coming over for lunch."

Lupe gets a spoon and tastes a meatball from the sauce pan.

"The meatball tastes very good but this is not the way I make meatballs. I mix pork, veal and beef in the meatball. You made these with only beef."

"Yeah, well I found the chopped beef in the freezer and used it."

"Frankie, are you OK? I never saw you cook anything before. You only make coffee or tea. Now you only make coffee? Where did you learn to make sauce and meatballs?"

"I learned by watching Tyler Florence make meatballs on television last night. That's where I got the idea. Tyler used pork, veal and beef just like you do. But I only had chopped beef."

Lupe says, "I shall make salad and some garlic bread, then set the table. I'll cook the spaghetti when the police officers arrive."

Frank pours her a cup of coffee. "Sit down, have a cup of coffee first."

Lupe looks at Frank and thinks his head is not quite right yet.

At noon time on the corner of Sutton Place and East Fifty-Sixth Street, FBI Special Agent Danny Johnson shakes the hand of his half-brother, Detective Lieutenant Louis Rodriguez. Danny is a large, muscular man with light brown skin. He is thirty-eight years old.

Danny tells Louis, "I emailed you the background information on Burke's employees this morning. The young administrative assistants are all clean. They are excellent

James Cage

students. The associate partners and assistant traders have no police records. Sam Nunn has a law degree and passed the bar. Sam is black but I bet he is mixed like I am. Richard Stanley is a CPA and upstanding citizen. John Burke is also clean. But this is an interesting fact. John Burke's father's name was Yuri Buchenco. Yuri is a real estate broker with possible connections to the Russian mob. He is seventy-six years old and works in his uptown Manhattan office every day. Yuri changed the family name to Burke before his son was born. John Burke was born in Brighton Beach, Brooklyn but brought up in Manhattan. Richard Stanley, Burke and Rosseus went to NYU together. Frank Rosseus is our age and a few years younger than Stanley and Burke. Frank was pushed ahead in school. He was only sixteen years old when he was a freshman at NYU. Richard Stanley, John Burke and Frank Rosseus have been close friends for over twenty years."

"What about the head trader Alan Sinclair?"

"He was born in Toronto, Canada in 1947. His family moved to New York State when he was a child. He attended undergraduate college at Elmira, New York. In the late 1960's Sinclair completely disappeared off the grid until 1987, when he enrolled at Temple University in Philadelphia. Sinclair received a PHD in computer science in 1991. He was forty-four years old. He was a trader for his own company in Newport Beach, California. He had other investments in small businesses and real estate. Sinclair is a millionaire. He was married and divorced in the late ninety's, no children."

"Interesting," Louis nods at the apartment building. "Let's go upstairs and meet Frank."

Louis and Danny tell the concierge they are visiting the Rosseus apartment on the eleventh floor. The concierge takes one look at them and knows they are cops. "Take the elevator," he says. He does not ask them to sign the guest book.

Danny and Louis enter the lift. There is no music. They exit the elevator and ring the bell to Apartment 11-A. They realize that there are only two large apartments on the floor. Apartment 11-B is down the hall.

At seven minutes after twelve noon, I hear the bell and open the door. Louis and the FBI agent walk in. The FBI man is taller and broader than Louis. "Would you guys like to see the apartment?"

Detective Louis Rodriguez says, "I'd like to introduce you to FBI Special Agent Danny Johnson,"

We shake hands and I introduce them to Lupe.

I walk my guests through the apartment. The apartment has three bedrooms, three and a half baths, a kitchen, living room and office-den. There is gym equipment in the office-den, barbells, dumbbells, loose weights, a bench with a barbell and a Pro-Form treadmill. There is a small table with a laptop computer and printer/scanner. A wall is covered by a large bookcase filled with books. I am not sure what the books are about.

Danny says, "Don't you belong to a gym?"

"Yes, I belong to a gym downtown near my office. But on weekends I workout at home."

Louis and Danny sit down at the dining room table. Each place setting has water and wine glasses, a salad dish, bread dish and a large plate for the spaghetti and meatballs plus all necessary utensils.

Danny says, "What are we having for lunch?"

"Spaghetti and meatballs," I answer.

Louis says, "A perfect meal for Memorial Day."

I go into the kitchen and carry back a large salad bowl. Lupe brings in hot Italian garlic bread. We all sit down to eat salad and bread.

We make small talk. Lupe tells the guys where she is from in Mexico and how long she has worked for the Rosseus family. I tell them I am feeling much better. The guys tell me they are half-brothers. They have the same father. I don't ask why they have different last names.

After the salad is finished, Lupe clears the used plates. I go to the kitchen and bring back the spaghetti Lupe has prepared. Lupe follows with a dish of twenty medium sized meatballs.

The two policemen are very hungry. They dig right into the pasta and meatballs.

It is obvious these men had not eaten anything earlier, so I ask, "Are you guys married?"

Danny says, "I was engaged a few years ago but my fiancé broke the engagement. She married a lawyer. They live in Chicago."

Louis says, "I am divorced and have one daughter. My little girl, Jennifer is four years old. My wife is presently a college professor at a small mid-western school. She remarried three years ago. She did not like my job as a New York City Police Officer."

Danny speaks, "Frank we would like to interview your partners. Can we meet them at your office, say Thursday the thirty-first of May?"

"Sure, I'll arrange the meeting for early morning, around 8:30 AM."

Louis looks at Danny and says, "That will be fine."

When the guys get up to leave, Lupe asks, "Detectives, did you enjoy the meal?"

Louis says, "The spaghetti and meatballs where delicious. The meal reminded me of the Italian food our father used to make."

Danny adds, "Except the meatballs were made only with beef, the old man used beef, veal and pork."

Lupe smiles.

Tuesday, May 29

I read in Tuesday's New York Times May 29, 2012 page five the following report. *"During the Memorial Day holiday, Monday, May 28, 2012 at approximately 11:00 AM, the charter fishing boat Charlene III blew up about five miles off the coast of Montauk Point. Skipper Charles Monsetti, crew members Jimmy Dolan and Mike Delpino and guests John Burke, his wife Marlene and twin daughters, Christine and Georgette; his business partner Richard Stanley and his wife Jean-Marie and two sons Peter and Paul were all killed in the accident. A US Coast Guard investigator stated, "A fuel leak caused the explosion. It was a catastrophic accident."*

I cannot believe what I just read. It is 6:30 AM and I am drinking Café Americano. I get the call. It is from Louis.

"Can Danny and I meet you as soon as possible at your downtown office?"

"I'll jump in a cab and be there. Where are you, detective?"

"We are at the FBI center a few blocks from the Burke Partners Broadway office. We shall walk over."

Before I leave, I read the New York Times article again. Out loud I say, "Fuck."

Would Frank Rosseus say, Fuck?

No, he would not. Frank was not a crude and vulgar man. "I rented a pay for view video last night, *The Girl with the Dragon Tattoo*. There is a scene in Stockholm, Sweden at the apartment of the female protagonist Lisbeth Salander. Lisbeth wears a tee shirt that says, *Fuck You, You Fucking Fuck*. I figure Lisbeth Salander must live in a section of Stockholm, Sweden similar to Newark, New Jersey. I think, *Fuck You, You Fucking Fuck*, is the state logo for New Jersey written in a *Mad Magazine* article decades ago. I checked this out on the Internet but could not find the article. Anyhow, when the movie was over, I went online at Amazon and ordered the tee shirt.

During the taxi ride downtown, the controller tries to send me psychic guidance. These signals are screwing up my head. I am upset. I have to read the book on meditation as soon as possible so I can calm down the limbic system and shut out the signals. I need to relax the mind of Frank Rosseus.

When I arrive at Frank's office, Detectives Louis and Danny are waiting there. We enter the main trading room. The detectives introduce themselves to all six traders present: Loren Holmes, Samuel Nunn, Lucille Ortega, Peter Murzenski, Keith Sprague, and Dr. Alan Sinclair. A few minutes later the administrative assistants enter the office: Janice DeMarco, Carolyn Murphy and Andrew Moreno.

Louis looks over the three young people. "I am Detective Louis Rodriguez. This is my colleague FBI Special Agent Daniel Johnson. Did you read this morning's New York Times?"

Janice DeMarco answers, "Yes we have."

"We will ask you a few questions a bit later."

The three young people look at me. I say, "Take work slowly today and keep things organized."

Louis and Danny follow me into Frank's private office.

Danny says, "Give me a breakdown of the offices and personnel."

"The office to my right is John Burke's office and Richard Stanley's office is to my left. Upon entering the company we are in the main trading area. The first cubicles are for the three administrative assistants. Janice works directly with John Burke. Andrew is a new CPA and works with Richard Stanley. Carolyn works with me. The large back office is Alan Sinclair's. He is supervisor in charge of all the traders. Loren Holmes is his assistant in the cubicle next to him. Peter Murzenski works with his assistant trader Sam Nunn. Keith Sprague works with his assistant Lucille Ortega. You can see the ticker screens for US: S&P 500, NASDAQ, DOW, Oil, Ten year bond, EUR/USD and Gold. The European screens are: FTSE 100, DAX and CAC 40. Asia displays are Nikkei 225, Hang Seng and Strait Times."

Louis says, "We checked out all your employees and everyone has come up clean."

I add, "We run background checks before we hire anyone."

Danny says, "Do you use private investigators?"

"Yes, we use Lydda Security. They are located in Long Island City across the East River in Queens. They also own a large security guard complex in Lincroft, New Jersey."

Danny responds, "Who recommended Lydda Security?"

"Lydda was recommended by John's father Yuri."

"Did you know John's father is Russian?"

I answer, "Actually Yuri is Ukrainian. I know his last name was Buchenco before he changed it to Burke a long time ago."

Louis asks, "What happens to Burke Partners after the deaths of John Burke and Richard Stanley?"

"The partnership is automatically dissolved. Alan Sinclair and I are the only general partners left. I have to consult with Alan. We will probably sell the trading programs and close the firm."

Danny questions, "Did you have any disgruntled employees who quit the company?"

"No, we add people as we need them. Our employees come highly recommended. Because we give bonuses to all employees, no one has quit. We give the administrative assistants bonuses every Christmas. For example Carolyn Murphy and Janice DeMarco are the newest and youngest workers. They start at fifty thousand dollars per year and each receives a bonus of fifteen thousand dollars at the end of the year. Andrew Moreno is now a CPA and makes sixty-five thousand dollars yearly plus a bonus of twenty thousand dollars. Our youngest assistant trader Loren Holmes makes one hundred fifty thousand dollars per year plus a thirty thousand dollar bonus. Lucille Ortega's salary is two hundred thousand dollars plus a forty thousand dollar bonus. Samuel Nunn makes more in salary because he gives in-house legal advice. Sam's salary is two hundred thirty thousand dollars per year plus a fifty grand bonus. Their salaries are secure. The forecasted bonuses will be honored. Peter Murzenski and Keith Sprague make at least a million dollars apiece plus a percentage of the profits. Alan Sinclair, John Burke, Richard Stanley and I receive twenty percent each of profits after all

James Cage

employees are paid and given bonuses. Ten to fourteen percent of profits are invested in the firm for research and development and we retain cash on hand for any emergency. I told this to Detective Rodriguez last week. Accept I failed to mention something. We have a few private investors in the firm. They are Yuri Burke, Dr. Paul Sinclair, the brother of Alan and George Foster Richmond the owner of Lydda Security. Of the eighty percent share from the full partners, twenty-percent or five percent from each full partner is returned to the private investors as cash dividends."

Danny says, "So every full partner really receives fifteen percent of the profits. And the three investors split twenty percent."

"Yes, each investor receives slightly more than six and one half percent of the profits."

"Can we speak with Sinclair now?" asks Louis.

I wave to Alan Sinclair. He sees me and comes to my office. I pull down the blinds so we are out of sight from the other workers.

The two policemen had previously introduced themselves to Alan.

I ask, "Alan when do you want to sell the trading programs and close the company?"

Alan says, "I think we should close up shop as soon as possible. We can use Sam Nunn as our lawyer to liquidate the firm."

"Have you been threatened by anyone Dr. Sinclair?" asks Danny.

"This past weekend when I was in New Jersey, two men in a Dodge Ram tried to run me off the road around 12:30 AM. But they blew a tire and went into a ditch. I drove away as fast as I could."

Louis asks, "What kind of car do you drive?

"I drive a Porsche Boxster S."

Danny says, "You can get away quickly from anyone on the road with that Porsche."

"Exactly," answers Alan Sinclair.

Louis speaks, "How did you come to work for this company Dr. Sinclair?"

"I am an old friend of Yuri Burke. He told me his son and college buddies wanted to open a stock trading firm. Yuri felt a more experienced trader and computer software engineer was needed to guide the new business. That's how I became involved with the company."

"Did you have prior business dealings with Yuri Burke?

"Yes, we did a few real estate deals together."

I am getting bored with the interrogation of Alan Sinclair. I walk to the back of Frank's office and turn on this strange looking radio. I press a button and music plays softly. Wilson Pickett is singing *Mustang Sally.* I sing, "You better slow your Mustang down."

Danny, Louis and Alan turn around to look at me. Danny and Louis are surprised that I am singing. Alan smiles.

I turn off the radio. Then I ask Alan, "Please tell the others that we are closing the firm."

Alan says, "I'll suspend all trading and tell everyone to make preparations to clear out their files."

Danny says to Alan, "Tell the employees to stay here today. Louis and I need to interview them."

Alan departs from Frank's office. He announces over the speaker to suspend trading and take a break. He asks Loren Holmes and Lucille Ortega to pick-up coffee and donuts. After the coffee break, the workers return to their individual cubicles. Alan, Louis, Danny and I enter Frank's office. I think, "Frank's office is my office but it really is not."

Next, every employee is individually called into Frank's office and interviewed by Louis and Danny. Alan and I remain for all the interrogations. The detectives ask the same basic questions. "Have you been threatened, followed or harassed by anyone over the past few weeks? Where were you on Memorial Day weekend?"

Everyone answers, "No," to the first question. Then they give the detectives their locations during Memorial Day Weekend.

Danny and Louis enjoy interviewing the attractive young women: Loren, Lucille, Janice and Carolyn. I can tell the girls like the two handsome detectives.

After Danny and Louis depart, Alan and I meet with the entire firm. We tell them they have until the first of July to clean out all files. They can take their time closing up shop.

Alan tells Peter Murzenski and Keith Sprague they will receive a million dollars each severance pay and additional money when the trading program and algorithms are sold. An educational trust fund will be set up for their children."

Peter and Keith shake hands with Alan and me. They say they want to take a few days off and will return next week to close things out.

I tell the young employees: Loren Holmes, Lucille Ortega, Samuel Nunn, Andrew Moreno, Janice DeMarco and Carolyn Murphy that they will receive their full salary and bi-monthly paychecks for the rest of the year. They will also get Christmas bonuses.

Then I state, "You are highly intelligent individuals with stellar academic credentials. You are all very young, under thirty years of age. There is a pre-med program at Columbia University that takes one year to complete. You can take pre-medical requirements and prepare for the MCAT exam. The firm will pay for the school year. When you get into medical school our education trust fund will pay your tuition for the entire four years. More doctors will be needed in the future because of the government socialized medicine program. A medical career is something to consider. There are a number of other education options. Some of you already have MBA degrees. We will pay for a PHD program. For Carolyn and Janice we have funds for any MBA, Masters or PHD program you wish to enter. Alan and I want you to have the best future possible. We may be able to arrange for you to have jobs in the finance and trading industries. Each of you can phone or email me or Alan and tell us how we can help. Alan and I will keep the office open until August 1, 2012."

After the staff leaves Alan and I have a discussion. Alan asks me, "How do you know about the pre-med program at Columbia?"

"I read about it on the Internet last week. It is called the Columbia University Post Baccalaureate Premedical Program and is the oldest program of its kind in the United States."

"A very good idea," answers Alan Sinclair.

"When will you contact the firm that is interested in purchasing our trading program?"

"I'll make the phone call now," says Alan.

It is 5:00 PM. Louis and Danny are enjoying a hamburger, French fries and beer at a local diner off Broadway.

"How do you like that Lucille Ortega?" asks smiling Danny.

"When you went to the restroom, I gave her a call. I'm meeting her for coffee tomorrow morning. I want to question Ms. Ortega about the partners," says Louis.

Then Louis says, "What do you think of Dr. Alan Sinclair?"

Danny answers, "Sinclair knows the firm is in some kind of danger. Both he and Frank will close the company almost immediately. They obviously have a buyer for the software program. Did you know Sinclair has a carry permit for a firearm in New York City?"

"Yeah, he has the permit because he carries large sums of cash," says Louis.

"I will arrange to interview him again," says Danny.

The Cowboy Wednesday, May 30

It is 3:00 AM, Wednesday the thirtieth of May. I finally finish the book on meditation techniques. I try to relax and focus. The entity is in the room. The Cowboy wears his hat. He smokes a Baronet cigarette.

The Cowboy speaks, "I needed to visit you. You have not allowed telepathic communications between us to be processed in the mind of Frank Rosseus. You know I am your controller."

"I know that you are my controller but exactly who are you?"

I am a traveler in time, space and dimension. My name is Arturus Verturus."

Arturus Verturus reads my mind and says, "I know what you are thinking."

"What am I thinking?" I ask.

"You are thinking, why I am smoking Mexican cigarettes."

"Exactly," I answer. Then I say, "What place or dimension are you from?"

"I come from another dimension called the Boareen Rife or Rift. My purpose is to watch, report and protect beings. I was requested by The Chairman to guide you. Do you understand your assignment? You seem befuddled."

"I know and understand my job. However sights and sounds are confusing. I have problems filtering information. I feel that my past life affects my thoughts, judgments and reactions."

Arturus says, "Do you know who you really are, Jaime?"

"Yes, I am not Frank Rosseus."

Arturus speaks again, "Frank is a pure and kind spirit and has moved on to a higher plan of existence. He should have lived a long and prosperous life as a human being here on Earth."

I tell Arturus the Cowboy, "Before I die, part of my assignment is to put Frank's money to good use. With the help of Alan Sinclair and the young lawyer Sam Nunn, an educational scholarship trust fund is being established for the immediate group of associates and employees at the firm. Frank has a last will and testament. He leaves money to

Guadalupe and her family. He has a number of educational institutions in the will. Frank donates money to St. Jude's Children's Hospital in Memphis, Tennessee. I'll add Beth Israel Hospital to the list and a large sum of money for the educational trust fund." I finally say, "Why are you smoking Mexican cigarettes?"

"Because I thought you might like one?"

Arturus the Cowboy flips a hard pack of Baronets over to me. I catch the pack and say, "Frank doesn't smoke."

Arturus Verturus puffs on his cigarette and in cloud of smoke he disappears.

Through the partially opened blinds, morning light enters my bedroom. I can hear Lupe in the kitchen. She is making coffee. The clock shows 8:00 AM. I get out of bed and say to myself, "What happened last night? Was that part of my reality or just a weird nightmare?"

I rub my face and look about the room. A hard pack of Baronet Cigarettes con filtro lies on the coffee table. Lupe walks into my bedroom. She says, "It smells like cigarette smoke in here." She looks at the coffee table. "Where did you get Mexican cigarettes? You have not smoked since you were a teenager. What's up?"

"Someone gave these to me and I only smoked one."

"Try to keep it down to three cigarettes a day. I made oatmeal and café con leche. Let's have breakfast," orders Lupe.

It is 9:00 AM. Louis Rodriguez sits in the window of Starbucks on Columbus Avenue and West Seventy-Third Street. Lucille Ortega lives on West Seventy-Third Street and wanted to meet at this location. Louis watches as she enters the coffeehouse. Lucille is a beautiful young woman. She is tall and slim with perfect facial features and green eyes. Lucille is half Puerto Rican and half Swedish. Her skin is as fair as Louis's.

She waves to Louis and proceeds to order a Cappuccino Grande. She walks over to his table sits down and says, "What are you drinking detective?"

"An espresso doppio."

"So you like to get charged up in the morning Louis?"

"I want to keep sharp," answers Detective Lieutenant Louis Rodriguez.

Lucille says, "I usually drink coffee in this Starbucks on weekends. It feels funny being here on a weekday. Well, let's get to the point Louis, what do you want to know about Burke Partners?"

"How long have you worked for the firm, Lucille?"

"I've been working for the firm since I graduated from Hunter College in 2007. I started as an assistant office administrator. After six months, Frank Rosseus and John Burke urged me to apply to the Stern School of Business at NYU. They cut my working hours to part time so I could attend the university full time. I received a partial scholarship and the firm paid for the other half of my tuition. They also continued to pay me full salary."

"When did you receive your MBA degree?"

"May, 2009; I graduated from NYU."

"How many people were with the firm when you started?" asks Louis.

"Only the partners and associates: Burke, Rosseus, Stanley, Sinclair, Murzenski and Sprague. I was the first employee."

"Who replaced you when you went back for your degree?"

"No one replaced me. Richard Stanley did all of the accounting work. Frank and John Burke took care of the office while Dr. Sinclair, Murzenski and Sprague did the trading. I worked Monday and Thursday from 9:00 AM to 1:00 PM. I also worked Friday afternoon from 1:00 PM till 5:00 PM."

"Who was the next employee?"

"They recruited Sam Nunn in 2008. He was a lawyer for one year at a firm and did not like it. Sam works with Peter Murzenski. They work well together."

"Are there any internal office conflicts?"

"No, which may seem hard to believe? We are too busy following the markets, trading and developing strategies. If there are differences of opinion Dr. Sinclair makes the final decision."

"Have you noticed changes of any kind with your colleagues? Are they more stressed, have personal problems, anything like that?"

"Everyone seems as usual except Frank."

"How is Frank different?"

"I have known Frank Rosseus for five years. He is a kindly man. He never gets angry. But he has changed since the accident. He is not as intense and totally focused. He came into the office for a few days last week. He sings softly to himself. Something he never did before the accident."

Louis says, "He had head trauma which probably affects his personality."

"I guess that's it," replies Lucille.

Louis questions, "What about office affairs. All the young women in the company are very attractive."

John and Richard were family men. Peter and Keith Sprague are also solid family men. Sam Nunn was married last year and has a baby on the way. Frank had a girlfriend but she left him a few years ago. He lost interest in relationships after that."

"I can understand that," says Louis.

"Why's that detective?"

"My wife divorced me a while back. She did not like the idea that I was a New York City Police Officer."

"Do you have any children?"

"Yes a daughter Jennifer."

"Where are your wife and daughter now?

"She moved to the mid-west with Jennifer and a new husband?"

"Oh, sorry," says Lucille.

"The marriage was over a long time ago," states Louis. Then he adds, tell me about Alan Sinclair."

"Dr. Sinclair is the brain behind trading strategies. He developed the computer algorithms and trading software."

"Does Sinclair have any relationships with women?

"I occasionally have dinner with Dr. Sinclair. He says he is too old to get involved with younger women. He was divorced back in the late 1990's. He is good company, a very interesting and learned man."

"Would you like to have dinner with me Ms. Ortega?"

"I certainly would Detective Rodriguez. By the way, where do you live Louis?"

"I live on East Eighty-Third Street, a couple of blocks from Central Park."

The Sinclair Interview Thursday, May 31

At 2:00 PM, Thursday the thirty-first of May, Special Agent Danny Johnson rings the bell of a brownstone building on West Eighty Second Street between Columbus Avenue and Amsterdam Avenue. Alan Sinclair says, "Come on up, I'm on the third floor."

Sinclair opens the door for Danny. "Sorry you had to walk up but this is an old building. I have the entire third floor to myself. Feel free to inspect the apartment, while I make some coffee."

Danny questions, "Who else lives in this building?"

Sinclair answers, "Guadalupe Gomez owns the first floor apartment, my brother Paul owns the second floor and I have this top floor."

"Where is your brother?"

"He lives in Wall Township, New Jersey where he is a surgeon. I visited him Memorial Day Weekend. He keeps this apartment in the city. I am sure you checked this out."

"Yes, I have but I still need to ask you some questions," says Danny.

Danny walks through a large living room and dining room. The apartment has two bedrooms and a spacious study. There is one photograph on the desk in the study. It is the only photo of actual people in the entire apartment. The other photos are outdoor scenes and pictures of birds in flight. Danny picks up the photograph from the desk. The picture is of three young men. He takes a closer look.

Sinclair calls him, "Detective the coffee is ready."

Danny walks into the kitchen and sits down.

"How do you like your coffee detective?"

"A little milk and a little sugar," says Danny.

"Tell me, Dr. Sinclair, about the incident on the road in New Jersey."

"Some nut nudged me off a back road in the dark. I think the driver was drunk."

Danny says, "What is really going on with the deaths of your partners?"

Sinclair answers, "The boating incidence is listed as an accident, am I correct?"

"Yes. But there is something else happening here."

"May I speak off the record?"

"Sure, I am not writing anything down or recording you."

"Last month John Burke, his father Yuri, Frank Rosseus, Richard Stanley and I had a meeting at Yuri's real estate office uptown on Madison Avenue. Yuri said a group of businessmen wanted to purchase Burke Partners and that the group was funded by the Russian Mafia. We would have to sell them the business. I voted to sell the business immediately but John, Frank and Richard refused to give up the company."

Danny says, "Frank had a near fatal accident. John Burke, Richard Stanley and others were blown up on a fishing boat. And you were run off the road."

Sinclair says, "Frank and I are selling the company to the Russians. We don't want any more accidents."

"So, Dr. Sinclair, you are going to let this mob get away with murder."

"Yes, the NYPD and FBI will not be able to prove anything."

Danny says, "You are telling me the FBI and the NYPD are never going to be able to prove the boating accident was murder and the hit and run on Frank was attempted murder."

"Yes."

Danny just shakes his head. He knows what Alan Sinclair has stated is true.

Alan pours Danny some more coffee. Danny adds milk and sugar.

"When will you and Frank finish shutting down Burke Partners?"

I contacted the interested party yesterday. The formal sale will be completed by the end of next week. Frank and I will keep the office opened until August 1, 2012."

Danny finishes his coffee. He shakes hands with Alan. "Thank you Dr. Sinclair. You've been very helpful. May I ask you about the photograph on the desk in your den?"

"Sure, says Alan."

"The three men in the photo are all young. The one on the left is you and the one on the right looks like it may be your brother?"

"Yes, that's my younger brother Paul."

"You all have shotguns. Where and when was the picture taken?"

"The photo was taken in Guatemala, August, 1971. We were pheasant hunting."

Then Danny asks, "Who is the young man in the middle?"

"A friend, he died a while back."

"Thanks," says Danny.

Yuri Buchenco alias Yuri Burke Friday, June 1

FBI agent Danny Johnson collected the background information on Yuri Burke.

Yuri Buchenco was born in 1936, outside Kiev, Ukraine. His father was Eastern Orthodox Catholic and his mother was Jewish. His father was killed during the Nazi invasion of the Ukraine in the summer of 1941. The mother and five year old Yuri were smuggled out of Eastern Europe into Italy. They lived in the Jewish Ghetto of Rome and eventually immigrated to Palestine. When Yuri was thirteen years old, they moved to Brooklyn, New York in March of 1949.

It is Friday afternoon, the first of June. Danny Johnson and Louis Rodriguez sit across a desk from Yuri Burke in his real estate office on Madison Avenue near Eighty-Seventh Street.

Louis says, "Mr. Burke do you know who is responsible for the death of your son and his family?"

Yuri answers, "The paper said it was an accident, let's leave it at that."

Danny adds, "We feel this was not an accident. Don't you want us to track down these murderers?"

"No, there is nothing you can do. Forget about this. Please release any remains of my son and his family as soon as possible so I can give them a proper burial."

Danny and Louis understand that this man is not going to talk.

Louis says, "Thank you for your time. We are sorry for your loss. We'll get your son and family's remains back to you."

Three Months Later Friday, August 31

It is 11:00 PM, the thirty-first of August. There is a large blue moon out tonight. I am on the hard line kitchen telephone with Alan Sinclair. I left the television on in the living room. I was watching *Reservoir Dogs*, a Quentin Tarantino film. The voice of Steven Wright announces a song by Stealers Wheel. I can picture Michael Madsen, as Mr. Blonde, singing and dancing around the room while he tortures a captive policeman.

I sing into the phone, "Clowns to the left of me."

"What's that," says Sinclair.

"Nothing, I'm just singing."

At 11:30 PM, The Cowboy, Arturus Verturus appears. He removes the cowboy hat and speaks to me.

"How are things going?" says Arturus.

"We have straightened out a lot of stuff over the past three months. Alan Sinclair sold the computer program to a Russian trading company. They paid only two million dollars for the program but we managed to negotiate an extra two and one half percent fee for the next five years."

"How does that work?"

I answer, "We get two and one half percent of their gross trading profits. They should easily earn one million dollars per week for fifty weeks. Therefore, two and one half percent of fifty million dollars equals one and one quarter million dollars per annum. Over a five year period we will earn six and one quarter million dollars."

Arturus asks, "Where will that money go?"

"The money goes into the Burke Partners Educational Trust Fund. All former partners, employees, associates, investors and their families will benefit. Frank Rosseus will donate a large sum of his personal money into this educational trust."

I stop to think about something from my past existence. I say, "I know you Arturus; you used to drive a taxi cab in Guadalajara, Mexico. You told me back then you watched and protected me. Are you St. Michael the Archangel?"

Arturus the Cowboy answers, "Yes I am Saint Michael but I am also Arturus Verturus from the Boareen Riff."

"Where have you been the last three months, Arturus?"

"I have left you alone so you can focus on your own. How is the meditation going?"

"My mind is clear," I answer.

"Tell me the status of your company employees and associates."

'Murzenski and Sprague work at a major trading firm in Jersey City, NJ. Loren Holmes will return to school for an advanced degree. She wants to get an Education Doctorate at Columbia University Teachers College. Loren will be a college professor. Lucille Ortega is enrolled in the pre-med program at Columbia University. Lucille will eventually become a doctor. Carolyn Murphy is returning to St. Johns University. She is in a PHD program in education. Janice DeMarco will attend the MBA program at NYU. Alan Sinclair and I have setup Sam Nunn in his own law firm. He will be handling the Burke Partners Educational Trust Fund. Sam will also be the executor of Frank's last will and testament. We started Andrew Moreno in his own accounting enterprise. His office is in the same downtown building as Sam Nunn's legal firm. Andrew will be doing all the accounting work for Alan Sinclair and Frank Rosseus."

"OK," says Arturus.

Arturus the Cowboy lights up a Baronet cigarette. He hands it over to me. I smoke the cigarette.

Arturus says, "The war in Syria will spread across Middle East. I will not get into religious dogma but war is punishment for the sins of man. By the way, love the tee shirt."

Arturus disappears. I look at my reflection in the mirror. I like the tee shirt too.

Saturday, September 1

Louis Rodriguez and Danny Johnson sit in their favorite uptown coffee shop on the West Side at Columbus Avenue and Eighty-Sixth Street.

Danny says, "We have come up with nothing in the Burke Partners investigation. The boat mishap is officially an accident."

Louis answers, "I know. The New York State Police and US Coast Guard's final report states the deaths of John Burke, Richard Stanley and others was an accident. The case is formally closed. But I doubt that Yuri Burke will let the death of his son go unpunished. He'll seek revenge."

Danny asks, "Did you ever track down the driver of the cab that struck Frank?"

"No, we hit a dead end. There was never a full description of the driver and we only have tapes of the cab hitting Frank."

Lucille Ortega walks into the diner and sits next to Louis across from Danny.

"So, I heard you are taking pre-med classes at Columbia," says Danny.

"Yes, I begin Tuesday morning the fourth of September," answers Lucille.

"Lucille there is a question I have been meaning to ask you and never got around to it."

"What is it Danny?"

"You know Alan Sinclair very well and you have been in his apartment a number of times. On the desk in the study, there is a photo of Alan, his brother Paul and another young man taken back in the early 1970's. Have you ever noticed the photograph?"

"Yes, I've seen it," says Lucille.

"The guy in the middle, does he remind you of anyone?"

James Cage

"Well, yes he does. When Frank Rosseus returned to work after his traffic accident, he was standing next to Alan. The photo came to my mind and I realized the guy in the middle looked like Frank."

Louis says, "What photo are you talking about?"

"I forgot to mention this to you Louis. When I visited Dr. Sinclair's apartment a few months ago I noticed a photo of three young men. The guy in the middle looked familiar to me. Come to think of it, he does look a lot like Frank," says Danny.

Danny takes out his cell phone and calls Alan Sinclair.

"Dr. Sinclair, this is Danny Johnson, how are things going?"

"Fine, what's up detective?"

"I am sitting in a diner with my brother Louis and Lucille Ortega. Can we see you? I want Louis to look at the photograph on your desk. We can bring you some breakfast."

"Come right over, just bring me coffee with milk," says Alan Sinclair.

In Sinclair's apartment Alan sits down with Lucille and drinks coffee. Louis follows Danny into the den; Danny grabs the photo from the desktop and hands it to Louis.

Louis takes a long hard look at the man in the middle then places the photo back on the desk.

"Thirty years younger but that's him," says Louis.

"Yeah, that's definitely him," answers Danny.

When they return to the kitchen, Alan Sinclair says, "Do you guys have the answers you were looking for?"

Danny responds, "Yes, we know the guy in the photo with you and your brother."

Lucille says, "Well who is he?"

Louis answers, "The person in the picture was killed in 2005. The case is an unsolved homicide. In 2007, when Danny became an agent with the FBI and I joined the NYPD we investigated the incident for a joint FBI, NYPD, New Jersey State Police task force. We came up empty. The guy in the middle was run over by a white van at the Metro Park Train Station in New Jersey on the twenty-first of May, 2005. The incident was recorded on videotape. The van and the driver were never found."

Lucille goes into the study and brings back the photograph. She says, "Frank is about forty years old but this is what he would have looked like at twenty years old. What is the connection here?"

Danny and Louis do not answer.

Alan Sinclair says, "That's Frank's father."

Lucille responds, "I've been at Frank's apartment with you Alan. Frank has shown me pictures of his father and mother. Frank's father looks nothing like this guy."

Alan says, "Frank was adopted, this is a picture of his real father."

Danny speaks to Alan Sinclair, "Does Frank know any of this?"

"Frank has seen the photograph but has never said anything about it."

"Alan would you call Frank and ask him to come over," says Louis.

When I arrive; Alan, Louis, Danny and Lucille are sitting at the kitchen table. Alan takes me into the den and hands me the photo.

I glance at the picture and put it down.

Alan asks, "You have seen this photo before. Do you know who these people are?"

"Yes, it is you and your brother Paul."

"Do you know the man in the middle?"

"Yes, it's me."

Alan takes a long, hard look at me. He knows who I am and that I have transmigrated into the body and soul of Frank Rosseus. "You can't tell them inside that this is you, Jaime."

"Just tell them, it's Frank's father because it is too, isn't it?"

"Yes," says Alan Sinclair.

James Cage

Tuesday, September 25

It is 10:00 AM, Tuesday the twenty-fifth of September. Alan Sinclair, Yuri Burke and a distinguished elderly gentleman sit inside the Midnight Express Diner on the corner of East Eighty-Ninth Street and Second Avenue.

Yuri Burke speaks to the old man, "Do we have clearance on this?"

"Yes," answers Lord George Foster Richmond.

George Foster Richmond than speaks to Alan Sinclair. "Kill those responsible for the murders of Yuri's son's family and the others. Do it anyway you can."

"My brother Paul and I will take care of it," states Alan Sinclair.

Yuri Burke says, "How much time do you have left, George?"

"I am ninety-six years old and still function well. But at this point in my life, I need a bodyguard twenty-four/seven. In all honesty, I don't care to live much longer."

"The big guy outside, that's your bodyguard?"

"Yes, he's a good kid very loyal, very intelligent. I have made him president of my security company Lydda," answers George.

Then George speaks to Alan Sinclair. "Tell me how Frank Rosseus has been doing since his accident. I have not seen him since last Christmas."

"He has hallucinations. He sings to himself. He thinks he is his father."

George says, "How can Frank think he is his father when he never knew anything about him?"

Sinclair answers, "There is a theory that DNA from the parents carries memories to the offspring. Perhaps brain trauma from the taxicab collision set off the father's memories within the mind of Frank."

George says, "I doubt the theory is valid."

Burke asks, "The two detectives, they are Frank's brothers?"

Sinclair answers, "Yes, they watch out for Frank. Danny, Louis and Lucille Ortega have dinner with Frank at least twice a week. And of course Guadalupe always takes care of him."

"My son and Frank were close friends for many years. But who is Frank Rosseus, really?" says Burke.

George answers, "Frank's mother was Guadalupe's sister. She died at childbirth. His birth father was one of us. The Rosseus family wanted to adopt a child. Frank's adoptive parents and Guadalupe set up the adoption through the Catholic Church. It worked out well. Frank had great parents and a good life. And he always had Aunt Lupe to take care of him."

Burke says, "George, I have to get back to work. I thank you and Alan for everything." Yuri Burke shakes hands with Alan Sinclair and George Foster Richmond. Yuri leaves the restaurant.

George says to Sinclair, "I had my bodyguard train Frank in the use of firearms from January through March. I wanted Frank to have a concealed weapons permit in New York and New Jersey. It may have been necessary for Frank to transport large amounts of cash in case anything happened to you. We spoke about this last Christmas."

"Yes, I remember. I thought it was a good idea back then but not now," says Alan.

George says, "I understand. Call Frank. I want to see if he remembers any of this."

Alan contacts me on his cell. "George Foster Richmond is here, he would like to see you. May we stop by?"

"Sure, come right over," I answer.

Sinclair and George leave the diner and walk over to the Cadillac parked outside. The bodyguard opens the back door. George says, "Alan, you have met Patrick a number of times."

"Good to see you again," says Alan.

Alan and Patrick shake hands. George and Alan Sinclair get into the back seat of the car. Patrick drives south on York Avenue toward Sutton Place.

Lupe opens the door and gives George and Alan a hug. "Would you like something to eat or drink?"

Alan answers, "No thank you Lupe, we just had breakfast."

Lupe brings Alan and George into the kitchen. I sit at the table. I get up and walk over to Alan and George and shakes hands.

George says, "You look well. It is good to see you again. Do you remember the last time we saw each other?"

I answer, "Yes, it was May 20, 2005 in Washington, DC."

Alan questions, "George, Paul and I had dinner with you at Divino's Restaurant a few days before Christmas last year."

"I don't remember that."

George studies me. He knows who I am. "Jaime, would you like to have dinner with Alan and me tonight?"

"Sure, what time?"

"I'll make reservations at Divino's for eight," says George.

I sing, "Dinner at eight," trying to sound like Frank Sinatra. George and Alan smile.

They leave the apartment. Inside the elevator, Alan Sinclair says, "Jaime saw you May 20, 2005, the day before he was killed in New Jersey?"

George answers, "Yes, May 20, 2005 was the last time I saw Jaime in Washington D.C."

I get to Divino's Restaurant at 8:00 PM sharp. There is a big Irish guy standing outside the restaurant. I go up to him and look him straight in the eye and say. "How are things going, Pancho? It is good to see you again. How long has it been, four years?"

Pancho takes a long hard look at me. "Shush," says Pancho. "I am Patrick Kelly. And the last time you saw me was in late March."

"Yeah, and I am Frank Rosseus."

Pancho says, "I am holding this body for the old man. When he dies, his soul will transmigrate into Patrick Kelly."

"George never really dies, does he?" I say.

"Only we die Jaime, over and over again."

I shake hands with Pancho Villa/Patrick Kelly and enter the restaurant.

All the tables are full. There are mostly couples. Some of the women are very beautiful. Within the restaurant, Alan and George sit at a table with a clear view of the sidewalk. On this warm, pleasurable Tuesday evening, they watch the Saturday night type Manhattan crowd walk by. I sit down between Alan and George the Bear.

Alan orders an inexpensive California Merlot. The waiter retrieves the wine and pours everyone a glass. I take a sip. The wine is good. Then George orders dinner for us; salad, veal chops and potatoes.

He says, "Alan and his brother Paul are going to take care of recent developments. You understand this, Jaime?"

"Yes, I do."

Alan speaks, "I see you recognize George's bodyguard Patrick."

"Yes, we've met before many times."

George states, "After diner, Patrick will drive you home. Alan and I have a little extra business to discuss."

"Ok," I answer.

Dinner arrives and we dig in. Alan orders another bottle of wine. Everyone in the restaurant seems to be enjoying the food. We make small talk. Alan tells George about our former employees. They are all moving forward on the path of life.

After dinner we have American coffee. I thank George for dinner, shake hands with Alan Sinclair and leave the restaurant.

I get into the Cadillac with Pancho. He says, "We have an assignment to complete."

I answer, "That's fine. Alan Sinclair knows who I am. I don't know if his brother Paul does?"

"Right now, only George knows everything and what we shall do."

Lucille Ortega's Apartment Tuesday Evening

Louis and Lucille walk through her apartment to the bedroom. They aggressively kiss and almost tear off each other's clothes. Lucille practically throws Louis onto her bed and gets on top of him. Louis lifts her up and flips her over. They make love wrestling and pulling at each other.

Back to the Cadillac

Pancho and I are in the limo driving south on FDR drive. Pancho says, "Jaime, open up the glove compartment."

I open the compartment and pull out a Smith and Wesson thirty-eight caliber, long barreled policeman's special. I check to make sure the gun is loaded. I also take out a silencer and attach it to the gun.

Pancho drives the Cadillac over the Brooklyn Bridge, we eventually get to Ocean Parkway, turn on Avenue P and park on Sixteenth Street.

Pancho and I exit the car. He carries the same weapon as I do. We conceal the guns under our jackets. We walk a few blocks and stop at a single family residence. Pancho surveys the area.

He says a prayer in Latin. *"Sancte Michael Archangele, defende nos in proelio contra nequitiam et insidias diaboli esto praesidium. Imperet illi Deus, supplices deprécamur: tuque, prínceps militiae caelestis, Satanam aliosque spiritus malignos, qui ad perditionem animarum pervagantur in mundo, divina virtute, in infernum detrude."*

I add, "Amen."

Pancho has a key to the house and opens the door. We walk through the home into the living room. A young man and woman recline on the couch. They peacefully watch a movie on television. Pancho and I shoot and kill them.

Back in the Cadillac, as we drive toward Manhattan, Pancho says, "Do you know who we just killed?"

"Yeah, the driver of the taxi cab that murdered Frank Rosseus."

Then Pancho says, "The girl had to go too?

"I know," I answer.

"Pancho, can you do me a favor?"

"You want me to send you a girl, don't you Jaime?"

"Yes, how much for a first class young woman?"

"Five grand, she'll be at your apartment by midnight. Clear it with security downstairs, so she can go right up."

"Do you remember my type?"

"Yes, she should be about twenty-four years old, around five six in height, blonde hair, blue eyes and perfect legs."

"And she shouldn't talk much," I add.

"You got it," answers my friend Pancho Villa/Patrick Kelly.

Frank's Apartment Bedroom

Directly in front of me, at the foot of Frank's bed, an exceptionally attractive young, blond woman stands. She is conservatively dressed in pants, blouse and light weight jacket. Her appearance is nothing like that of a prostitute. She looks like a university graduate student. She gently takes my face into her hands and softly kisses me.

I tentatively kiss her.

She takes control of the situation and makes purposeful, slow love to me.

Saturday, September 29

It is Saturday the twenty-ninth of September. It is 6:00 AM. I leave my apartment building. I take a taxi cab to Alan Sinclair's apartment on the West Side. He is waiting for me outside the building with the Porsche. I open the door and hop in. We are off to New Jersey, the Garden State.

Alan drives across town, goes through the Lincoln Tunnel, gets on the New Jersey Turnpike and turns south. He exits the turnpike and enters the Garden State Parkway, crosses the Driscoll Bridge and continues driving south for about thirty miles. We depart the parkway at exit 98.

As we exit the parkway I ask Alan, "What really happened when that truck tried to run you off the road last May?

"I shot out their front tire. Then I drove away."

James Cage

At 7:30 AM we arrive at the home of Dr. Paul Sinclair, on Robin Hood Drive in Wall Township. This is an upscale residential neighborhood with trees and manicured lawns. The house is situated on two acres of land. George's big, black Cadillac is parked in the driveway. Alan parks his Porsche behind the Caddy.

Alan rings the bell at the front door. Pancho opens it and we walk into the house. The main house contains a large basement with a small gym, den, business office, bedroom, kitchen and two bathrooms. The middle level of the house features a substantial living room, dining room, kitchen, bathroom, and maid's quarters with a separate bathroom. There are four bedrooms with private baths on the upper floor. A three car garage is connected to the main house with only a Mercedes Bens in one space. There is a swimming pool, garden and guest house in the back.

Paul Sinclair has given his maid the day off. In the kitchen, Paul prepares breakfast for George, Pancho, Alan and me. Bacon and eggs over easy, rye toast, coffee and orange juice. To cut down on the carbohydrates there are no home fried potatoes.

After breakfast we enter the dining room. Maps and other documents are neatly arranged on the large dining room table.

George says, "There are two operations. Alan will take care of the Russians that killed the Burke Partners. Paul will assist him. The other mission concerns four European men and one American. They will be visiting the estate of the American in Rumson, New Jersey sometime in late November or early December. Patrick and Lydda Security will handle that mission. Finally, Frank is executor of my estate. He will take care of my personal business."

I note that Alan Sinclair has been told of these operations. He completely understands the real identities of Pancho and me. His brother Paul senses the differences in Patrick Kelly and Frank Rosseus but has not spoken about it.

Tuesday, October 2

On Tuesday the second of October at 9:00 AM, Alan Sinclair walks into the diner at Columbus Avenue and Eighty-Sixth Street. He proceeds to a back booth and sits next to Louis Rodriguez across from Danny Johnson.

Louis says, "We know about George Foster Richmond. Danny and I had a business relationship with him a number of years ago. His FBI and CIA files are above Danny's security level."

Danny adds, "His personal bodyguard Patrick Kelly spends a lot of time with Frank. Did George Foster Richmond assign Patrick to protect Frank?

Alan answers, "Yes, George has Patrick watch Frank. As you know, George was an investor in Burke Partners and the owner of Lydda Security. He recently made Patrick Kelly president of Lydda. I have known George for many years. He is a very old man now. He is not a threat to anyone."

Danny says, "We have plenty of information on Patrick G. Kelly. He was born on Staten Island. Patrick is twenty-seven years old, six feet four inches tall and two hundred thirty pounds. His mother was a registered nurse. She died of colon cancer on May 5, 2011. His father was a New York City fireman who was killed when the twin towers went down on September 11, 2001."

Louis states, "Patrick attended Catholic schools. After his high school graduation in June 2003, he enlisted in the Navy. He was eighteen years old. He remained on active duty for six years. He is a Navy Seal. His military record is classified."

Alan replies, "Patrick recently graduated John Jay College of Criminal Justice this past May. He has a BA in Criminology. It took him only three years to complete the curriculum. Now he is President of Lydda Security where he has continually worked for over three years."

Alan stops talking and looks at Louis and Danny. They seem to be concerned about something. He says, "How can I help you detectives?"

Danny says, "We don't want any more attempts on our brother's Frank's life. Louis and I will look the other way. Do what is necessary to protect him."

Alan answers, "I shall."

Louis says, "Let's have breakfast."

Monday, October 29 Hurricane Sandy

It is Monday the twenty-ninth of October. It is 1:00 AM and there is an unseen full moon. Hurricane Sandy is hitting the New York, New Jersey area. I am smoking a Baronet cigarette with The Cowboy, Arturus Verturus.

Arturus speaks, "Jaime, give me a breakdown of the structure and strategy for the missions assigned by George Foster Richmond."

"The Bear mapped a vengeance strategy at Paul Sinclair's home last month."

"You still refer to George as The Bear?"

"Sometimes I do, yes."

Arturus says, "Tell me the plan."

"Alan and Paul Sinclair recruited a team of mercenaries from South Africa. They will do the job on the Russians that killed John Burke and Richard Stanley. Located in Miami Beach, Florida there is a yacht, Catherine the Great. The Russian Cartel, the Saint Petersburg Group, own the vessel. These men will set sail from Miami to San Juan, Puerto Rico on Wednesday, the seventh of November. The ship will be blown up before it ever makes port in San Juan."

Arturus the Cowboy says, "This is the vengeance that Yuri Burke seeks for the death of his son John?"

"I call the mission cold blooded murder. Innocent women, children and seamen will be killed because of the greed and avarice of a few men. But this is the game, 'An eye for an eye and a tooth for a tooth.'"

Arturus the Cowboy then says, "Didn't you and Pancho kill the taxi driver and his girlfriend last month? Isn't that cold blooded murder?"

I answer, "That's part of the assignment you authorized. We kill evil men and women."

He says, "You have another assignment, don't you?
"Yes."

Arturus the Cowboy smokes and thinks. "How was the young woman?"

"She was nice, her body felt nice." "I have a question for you. What happened to the real Patrick Kelly?"

Arturus the Cowboy, displays a vision on the wall.

Flashback Vision

There is a firefight in the mountains of Afghanistan. Patrick Kelly is shooting an M4 Carbine Rifle at an unseen enemy. Patrick gets hit and goes down.

Back to Present

Arturus explains, "Patrick Kelly was killed in the firefight in Afghanistan in the spring of 2008. He took a bullet in the gut. When he died on the operating table in Kabul, Pancho jumped in. He became Patrick and the body healed."

"Like when Frank Rosseus died on the operating table and I jumped into his body."

"That's right," answers Arturus the Cowboy.

"Did you know that Frank was my son?"

"Yes, that is why you were perfect for the assignment."

"I did not know I had a third son. When Danny, Louis and Frank were born, I was in Mexico. I didn't know Danny and Louis were my children until 1999."

"You were very busy in early 1973."

"After I returned to New York from Africa and Rome in December 1971 I got a job as a permanent substitute teacher. I taught at a Newark, New Jersey high school from January 1972 through June 1973. I returned to Mexico to go to medical school in the summer of 1973. Frank's mother was a young, pretty Spanish teacher. She was twenty-three years old and had just finished a relationship with someone. She liked me because I spoke a little Spanish and I was familiar with Mexico where she was born. I dated her a few times and only slept with her once. Her name was Sophia Gomez. I did not know she was Lupe's sister until I became Frank. It was only one time with Louis's mother and Danny's mother too. They all told me they took birth control pills. I did not use any protection."

"Obviously the pills did not work well back then."

"Before those young women, I just slept with hookers and used protection. I never wanted to be involved with emotional relationships."

"When did you know that Sophia Gomez died?"

When I got back from Mexico in December of 1973, a teacher acquaintance told me Sophia died. I did not know she died giving birth to my son."

I think a moment.

"Arturus, please tell me exactly what is going on. Pancho says a prayer to you, Saint Michael the Archangel before he goes into battle."

"I am the leader of the army of God. There is a war between good and evil constantly being fought within all dimensions of time and existence. You and Pancho are spiritually and genetically programmed to go back and forth from hell and purgatory to life on Earth to participate in these battles," answers Saint Michael/Arturus the Cowboy.

I ask, "What about George the Bear? What type of entity is he?"

"George slays dragons with me. He does not die. He will become Patrick Kelly when Pancho/Patrick dies."

"Where is the soul of Patrick Kelly?"

"Patrick's soul is in heaven with the soul of Frank Rosseus. They are both good and decent spirits."

Then Arturus adds, "Do you understand why you have become Frank Rosseus?"

"I have an idea. The employees at Burke Partners are special individuals. Frank's money will help them and their future families get a proper education and foundation. The four men: Peter Murzenski, Keith Sprague, Sam Nunn and Andrew Moreno will be major assets to society. The four young women: Janice DeMarco, Loren Holmes, Carolyn Murphy and Lucille Ortega have superior intellect and extraordinary compassion for human beings. They are great women."

Arturus says, "That is correct. There is a very evil hurricane arriving here." The entity smiles, a sad smile and disappears in a cloud of smoke.

Sunday, November 11

It is early Sunday morning the eleventh of November. Alan Sinclair relaxes at a private residence in Miami Beach. He flew down to Florida on Wednesday the seventh of November using an alternative identity Ward Jeffries. He reads an article on the back pages in the Sunday Miami Herald. The article states, *"The yacht Catherine the Great is missing at sea. The vessel was scheduled to arrive in San Juan, Puerto Rico on Saturday, November 10. A Coast Guard rescue team of aircraft and ships has been unable to find any trace of the ship."*

Alan's brother Paul did not accompany him to Florida the past week for a number of reasons. Hurricane Sandy caused massive destruction in coastal New Jersey. Paul, a surgeon, remained in New Jersey to treat patients in hospitals in both Ocean and Monmouth Counties. Many people were burned using gasoline generators, kerosene lamps and candles. Individuals were injured from flying debris. There were dead men, women and children in the morgues. They drowned in the ocean, rivers, bays and lakes. These deaths were not reported in the newspapers or on television.

Alan speaks on the telephone with his brother. He uses a telephone registered to Ward Jeffries. Paul's cell phone is billed to Arnold Benson another alias.

Alan says, "I'll be arriving at Newark Airport on United Airlines around 4:00 PM. I shall take a cab into New York. Drive my Porsche from your home. Take the Garden State Parkway to the New Jersey Turnpike through the Lincoln Tunnel into the city."

"Sure, answers Paul. "Is everything clear?"

"Get into town as early as possible. Call Yuri Burke from a public phone. Tell him everything is clear."

At 6:00 PM, Sunday the eleventh of November, I am in George's apartment on the northeast corner of East Seventy-Ninth Street and Fifth Avenue. Pancho has been living here with George. He has his own private bedroom and bathroom. Pancho, George the Bear and I sit at a large kitchen table overlooking Central Park.

George says, "My last will and testament is held by Sam Nunn at his downtown office. I sold my town house in London this past summer. The assets from Roslyn Genetics have been transferred to Molay Biotech Incorporated in Boston, Massachusetts. This apartment, all my businesses and part of my assets are willed to Patrick G. Kelly. I have two hundred million dollars in cash, stocks, bonds and securities. Eighty million dollars is gifted to hospitals, charities bio-medical and cancer research. Twenty million goes to the Burke Partners Educational Trust Fund. I want some of that education money for the children of employees of Lydda Security, as well as minority student college scholarships. Twenty million dollars is donated to Catholic schools and public higher educational institutions. There are fifty million dollars in a numbered Swiss bank account in the name of Patrick G. Kelly. There is ten million cash and securities located in a safety deposit box here in a New York City bank. The last ten million is stashed in a private bank off shore in the Cayman Islands. Everything is set. Frank Rosseus is executor of the will. Jaime, you will have access to all these assets. One of the purposes of your assignment is to make sure this transmigration of assets goes smoothly."

"What if I get killed on the mission with Pancho?"

"If anything happens to you, Alan Sinclair becomes executor of my estate."

We hear a slight swoosh sound. Arturus the Cowboy is in the room.

Arturus says, "You will be safe Jaime, I shall be watching you."

Arturus passes out Baronet Cigarettes. We all smoke.

Pancho says, "Jaime and I are going for a walk."

George and Arturus remain in the apartment.

Pancho and I walk down East Seventy-Ninth Street. Pancho touches the head of the statue, *El Gato,* near Park Avenue.

Pancho says, "What will you miss the most about New York City when we are back in hell?"

"I'll miss the women. I enjoy watching them run around Central Park."

"Did you miss viewing the marathon this year?"

"Not really because the hurricane was a devastating event. Louis Rodriguez told me the policemen and firemen refused to cover the marathon because there was so much damage to homes in Brooklyn and Queens. Their services were necessary to help the residents of the city."

We walk up Park Avenue and turn on East Eighty-Fourth Street. We stop at Starbucks on Third Avenue and order American coffee with milk. We sit down, peer through the window and gaze at the women strolling by.

When we return to the apartment Arturus the Cowboy is gone. George says, "Let's go over the mission. There are five primary targets. The location is Rumson, New Jersey. George goes to his brief case. He removes a security badge and identification and hands it to me. Jaime, this is your cover ID. You are an employee of Lydda Security."

I check the identification. My name is James Andrews. I look at George and smile sadly.

George says, "I don't want any mistakes."

Thursday, November 15

It is 8:30 AM, Thursday the fifteenth of November. Alan Sinclair and I sit across from Danny Johnson and Louis Rodriguez in their favorite booth at the diner on the corner of Columbus Avenue and Eighty-Sixth Street. The waitress pours four coffees.

Danny says to Alan, "A yacht, Catherine the Great, vanished in the Caribbean Sea last week. Some of the occupants were officials of the St. Petersburg Group. These people are all presumed dead. Wasn't it the St. Petersburg Group who purchased Burke Partners?"

"Yes," answers Alan.

Louis asks, "Do you know anything about the disappearance of this vessel?"

"No, I have no idea what you are talking about."

Danny says, "We checked your EZ-Pass records. On Tuesday morning the sixth of November you entered the New Jersey Turnpike at 7:05 AM. The final entry for that date is Exit 98 on the Garden State Parkway at 8:31 AM. There are other toll entries for the Garden State Parkway and Atlantic City Expressway on Friday the ninth of November. The final entries are for the New Jersey Turnpike and Lincoln Tunnel at 12:02 PM, Sunday the eleventh of November."

Alan answers, "I went down to my brother's place at the Jersey Shore to watch the election results Tuesday. I decided to stay for a few days. We took a daytrip to Atlantic City on Friday. We both came into New York on Sunday."

Louis says, "We spoke to Yuri Burke about this yesterday. He does not know anything about the missing yacht either."

I change the subject. I ask Danny, "I had dinner the other night with Louis and Lucille Ortega. Have you been seeing anyone lately?"

"No one special, but I received a call from your former employee Janice DeMarco. She is attending the MBA program at NYU. She is doing a research paper for a fraud and forensic accounting class. She wanted to know if I could help her get an interview with an FBI agent that works with forensic accounting. I told her yes. We'll meet for dinner tonight."

"Where?" asks Louis.

Danny says, "I'm not sure yet, I have to call her back."

Alan says, "Danny and Louis, you are invited to my brother, Paul's home in New Jersey for Thanksgiving. You can bring dates. Frank, Yuri Burke and George Foster Richmond will be there. You can ask us any questions you wish."

Louis speaks to me, "Would you like us to go to Paul Sinclair's for Thanksgiving, Frank?"

"Yes I would," I answer.

Danny and Louis look at Alan and me. They shrug their shoulders and answer, "Ok, we'll be there."

Danny says, "There won't be any more questions about the St. Petersburg Group or any of this."

Louis states, "An eye for an eye and a tooth for a tooth."

I say, 'Let's order breakfast."

Thanksgiving Day Thursday, November 22

It is 4:00 PM, the twenty-second of November, Thanksgiving Day at the home of Paul Sinclair, Wall Township, New Jersey. The guests are: Alan Sinclair, George Foster Richmond, Yuri Burke, Pancho Villa/Patrick Kelly, Louis Rodriguez, Lucille Ortega, Danny Johnson, Janice DeMarco and me. All the former employees of Burke Partners were invited but they had family commitments. Lupe Gomez was also invited but she went to Buffalo, New York to be with her daughter's family.

There is a large quantity of food. There are cheeses, bread, fruits, and nuts, various fancy vegetable dishes that contain asparagus, stuffed peppers, stuffed mushrooms and salads. There is Italian food, eggplant parmesan and stuffed shells with ricotta. The main course is turkey, stuffing, yams and green beans. There are pies: apple, pecan, mince and cherry. There are different wines mostly from California, red, white and rose. The horderves begin at 4:00 PM. The turkey dinner is served at 5:30 PM. Paul has his servers bring in a box of coffee from Dunkin Donuts. We have coffee and pie at 7:00 PM. Paul says all the leftover food will be brought to a homeless shelter.

Pancho and I sit together. We do not talk much. We watch the interactions between Danny and Janice, Louis and Lucille. George, Yuri and Alan relax and watch the football games. In the first game the Texans beat the Lions in overtime by a field goal. Paul is busy with his staff of four. The staff, two young women and two young men, work for Lydda Security. They serve food on fancy plastic dishes that are discarded. They take turns going outside for a cigarette and view of the street. Paul always gives his regular maid Thanksgiving Day weekend, Christmas, New Year's week, Easter week, the fourth of July and Labor Day off.

During coffee Lucille says to me, "Frank you seem to be like your old serious self."

"You mean, I don't sing to myself anymore?"

"Yes," She says.

Danny says, "Maybe it is not good for you to be so serious Frank. You were happier before."

"I am happy just being here for Thanksgiving with everyone."

Wednesday, November 28

It is just past midnight the twenty-eighth of November and there is a visible full moon. Arturus the Cowboy appears. He lights two Baronet Cigarettes and gives me one.

"What do you think about the wealth of information in the media?" he asks.

I have found that most of the news on television and in the newspapers is nothing but outright lies. I don't trust Internet websites; although some of their opinions may be true. Pancho tells me the Benghazi incident is total bullshit. George and Pancho are wired into the intelligence community. They say there isn't any American consulate in Benghazi. But there is a CIA operation centered in Libya that runs guns to rebels in Syria."

Arturus says, 'Most of the news that is reported is untrue, not even close to reality. In the United States, the media has become a propaganda arm of the administration. Europe is partly under the control of the men you will kill in Rumson, New Jersey. By eliminating them, the process of enslaving the people of Europe and the United States will slow down. What have you learned about these men, Jaime?"

"I know very little about the targets. Information on the Internet about these individuals is almost non- existent. May I have another cigarette?"

"Take the pack," says Arturus.

Around 8:00 PM, Pancho arrives at Frank's apartment for a late dinner. Lupe has stayed to prepare the meal. She makes salad, black bean soup, quesadillas and hot, spicy steak. Pancho has been at Frank's many times over the past few weeks. Lupe knows the big Irish guy Patrick loves Mexican food. We watch Bill O'Reilly on Fox News. The governor of Rhode Island has called the Christmas tree in the state house a holiday tree. When the governor speaks, Pancho/Patrick yells, "*Cabron*," and throws a tasty quesadilla at the television set. He hits the governor square on his television face.

Lupe says, "Nice shot."

We all have Mexican coffee and smoke Baronet Cigarettes after the meal.

Tuesday, December 4
At 5:15 AM, Tuesday the fourth of December, I take a cab over to George's apartment on Fifth Avenue and Seventy-Ninth Street. When I enter the apartment Pancho greets me.

He says, "George the Bear is not feeling well."

A registered nurse, an employee of Lydda Security, has been taking care of George since midnight. George Foster Richmond's body is failing. Before Pancho and I leave for New Jersey, I stop in George's room.

I say, "I'll do my job and take care of things."

"We'll see each other again," says George.

Pancho and I are in the Cadillac driving on the Garden State Parkway. We exit at Red Bank and head west. At 7:00 AM, we arrive at the Lincroft, New Jersey office of Lydda Security. Pancho parks the Cadillac in the large parking lot behind the building. Seven late model Ford E-Series commercial vans are stationed in the lot. There are a few Ford Taurus cars used for both transportation and surveillance. Other spaces are filled with employee vehicles.

We enter the two story building from a rear corner entrance. Pancho introduces me to the manager of the facility as James Andrews, a Lydda security officer from the New York City office. We go to Pancho's private office which takes up the entire backend of the building facing the parking lot. There is a room with a large desk and few files. There is a small kitchen and bathroom with a shower. An extra room with two sets of bunk beds has a full view of the parking lot.

Pancho says, "We shall stay here to prepare for this evening's mission. You can catch a nap in one of the beds. I'll have food brought in for breakfast and a late lunch."

I ask, "How many employees work here?"

"In this facility, ten administrative employees work around the clock. We have fifty security operatives from various backgrounds. Most are ex-military and retired state troopers who work as armed guards. We protect the homes of a dozen very wealthy families in Holmdel and Rumson."

"This place is much larger than the Lydda office in Long Island City," I say.

Pancho says, "In New York we provide mostly personal protection, bodyguard work, and surveillance and background checks. That's a 9:00 AM to 9:00 PM operation. As you know, Burke Partners employed Lydda to screen employees."

One of the staff brings in breakfast. Even though I drink some coffee, I fall asleep in one of the bunks. I wake up and look at the wall clock. It is 2:00 o'clock in the afternoon. I silently repeat the prayer in Latin to Saint Michael the Archangel.

It is 6:30 PM. Pancho and I arrive in a Lydda Security van at the Rumson estate. There are four armed Lydda security guards at the residence. Guard number one, from inside the gate house, opens the security gate. Pancho and I drive through. Pancho pulls the van in front of the residence. We are greeted by guard number two and guard number three. They escort us to the front door. Guard number two and guard number three remain stationed in front of the house. Pancho and I are armed. He carries the assault rifle and has a handgun tucked under his jacket. I have the Smith and Wesson revolver. I follow Pancho into the security room. Guard number four views the surveillance monitors. Pancho leaves the assault rifle in the security room. He then continues through the foyer of the house.

I watch Pancho on a video screen. He is greeted by the American owner and they shake hands. Pancho follows the owner into the kitchen and is introduced to the chef, his assistant, two women servers and two men servers. These people are not Lydda employees. The crew of cooks and servers are heavy security employed by the European guests to prepare and serve dinner. The group of young men and women are extremely fit and ready for action. They are armed. I can see guns that bulge slightly under the back side of their belts, covered by their jackets.

Guard number four says, "These servers are all armed. We did not check them for weapons because the owner told us not to. They must have set up in the bathrooms where we do not have any monitors."

I look at the kitchen monitor. Pancho touches his right cheek, a signal to take action.

Guard number four text messages the other three guards that the servers carry guns.

He says, "We have to take them out now."

Pancho does not waste time. When the chef and his assistant resume cooking and the owner and servers are relaxed, Pancho pulls his revolver and shoots the owner, the chef and the assistant chef in rapid succession. Guard number four and I pull our weapons and quickly move into the kitchen.

One of the young women servers is extremely fast, she moves, rolls, shoots and puts a bullet into Pancho's belly. Guard number four kills her immediately. The two male servers turn toward me, I shoot them both before they have time to draw their weapons. Pancho gets off his last shot and kills the other young woman. Her reaction time was too slow.

I and guard number four help Pancho into the security room. A bullet is lodged in Pancho's intestine. It will be a slow bleed and take him a long time to die. The bullet has to be removed. Pancho lies on the couch and I try to patch him up as best I can.

Guard number three arrives at the security room. He says, "We have a cleanup van standing by for emergencies like this. The van will be here in a few minutes.

At 6:58 PM a Lydda security van arrives at the estate. Guard number one allows the van to pass. The driver goes to the front of the house. He exits the van and opens the back door. He helps me, guards two, three and four load the seven bodies into the van. They are the American estate owner, chef, assistant chef, two women servers and two men servers. For easy loading and unloading the van has all back seats removed. The interior is covered with plastic. The bodies are covered with an extra layer of this dark plastic material. The driver leaves the compound to dispose of the bodies in a facility in Old Bridge, New Jersey about sixteen miles northwest.

The time is now 7:30 PM. I, guards number two, three and four return to the surveillance room. Pancho orders guards two and three to the roof of the house. Guard number four opens a closet. He removes two sniper rifles with suppressors and night vision scopes. He gives them to guards two and three. They depart for the roof.

Pancho tells me, "Grab a pair of night vision binoculars and go to the roof. Watch for the arriving guests and anyone else."

I go up to the roof. It is a warm, slightly misty night for December and comfortable to work outside.

At 7:45 PM two Cadillac limos arrive at the gate of the estate. Guard number one opens the gate and lets them in. The cars arrive at the front of the estate house. Everything has been cleared. When the two drivers and four guests exit the cars. Guard number three shoots and kills the first limo driver and European guest number one and guest number two. Guard number two immediately shots limo driver two and the other two Europeans numbers three and four.

From the roof, I scan the outside perimeter of estate with the binoculars. A Chevy Caprice is parked one hundred meters west of the front gate. I figure the occupants of this car are backup security for the Europeans. Although the shots were suppressed these men get out of the car. They sense something is wrong. They walk until they get to a side wall of the estate. One man boosts the other over the six foot wall. The man on the wall then helps the other one up. The two men are now inside the estate compound. I am not sure if guard number four in the security room has them on a monitor. Guards two and three have been too busy to notice the Chevy guys.

I tell guards two and three, "Two men have entered the compound over the western wall."

We come down from the roof and go into the security/surveillance room. Guard four has been watching a video screen. One of the Chevy men sneaks around the gate house. He shoots and kills guard number one with an automatic weapon. Guard number two runs out of the house. He sets himself in position. When the Chevy man leaves the gate house, guard number two shoots him dead with his rifle.

From the video camera stationed at the rear of the house, we can see Chevy man number two approach the house through the woods. Guard number three runs back up to the roof. We watch Chevy man number two get shot on the monitor. Guard number three is an excellent marksman. Pancho also watches this mess on the video screen. He tells guard number four to call Lydda security for another cleanup crew with four or five men. Some men will have to stay at the estate to thoroughly cleanup. That will take many hours.

Guard number two is now stationed at the front gate. When the van arrives with the cleanup crew he lets them in. There are eight more bodies that will be placed in a vat of acid at the Old Bridge facility. The two limo drivers, the four European guests and the two Chevy men. Guard number one will be cremated and his ashes dispersed. All the security guards assigned to this estate do not have families.

There will be no publicity or knowledge of this event. The American owner of the estate and the four European guests will die of natural causes at foreign locations on different dates.

James Cage

Their controlling group will prepare cover stories for them. The others will simply disappear off the face of the earth.

A total of sixteen people are killed on a warm December evening at a beautiful estate in Rumson, New Jersey. I am not really sure why?

I send a text message to Alan Sinclair about Pancho's condition. Alan sends me directions to bring Pancho, to his brother's medical facility.

I help Pancho get into the Ford van. He is still losing blood and getting weaker. I drive to Dr. Paul Sinclair's medical facility in Brick Township, New Jersey. The ride takes twenty five minutes.

Medical Building Brick Township, New Jersey

Alan Sinclair and I sit in the waiting room. The wall clock shows 9:35 in the evening. A half hour later, Paul Sinclair enters the room wearing surgical greens.

Paul says, "I took the bullet out, repaired the wound and transfused two pints of blood. For a moment Patrick stopped breathing. But a few seconds later, he came back to life. Frank you can speak to him in the recovery room."

In the recovery room, I take a hard look at Pancho Villa/Patrick Kelly. Pancho is gone. George the Bear is looking at me. I say, "Is that you, George?"

"Yes it is. And you can call me George. Patrick's middle name is George."

Arturus the Cowboy stands on the other side of the bed. He smiles then disappears.

When I leave the recovery room, Alan speaks to me. "I received a phone call from George's nurse. George died at 9:35 PM. She wants us to return to New York, as soon as possible."

Wednesday, December 5

At 2:00 PM on Wednesday the fifth of December, Alan Sinclair and I complete the legal work for the estate of Lord George Foster Richmond at the law office of Samuel Nunn.

Paul Sinclair has taken Patrick G. Kelly to his home in Wall Township. Patrick George Kelly will remain there with a nurse and Paul's maid for a few days. Paul will return to the city in the early evening and meet Alan and me at Divino's Restaurant.

It is 9:00 PM we order dinner at Divino's. Alan and Paul order arugula salad and veal Milanese. I have Caesar salad, spaghetti and meatballs. We drink two bottles of Merlot from the San Miguel vineyards in California.

Paul says, "Frank, how do you feel?"

"I feel tired. I don't want any coffee. I just want to sip the wine and relax."

Thursday, December 6

It is 7:58 AM, Thursday the sixth of December. I have just died in the body of Frank Rosseus. I am with Arturus the Cowboy. We are floating above the room. I hear Lupe open the door.

She calls, "Frank, Frank."

When there is no answer she comes into the bedroom. She touches Frank and finds the body to be warm. She immediately calls Alan and Paul Sinclair.

They arrive in fifteen minutes and come into the bedroom. Lupe is crying. Paul checks for a pulse.

"He's gone," says Paul. "They'll have to be an autopsy."

Alan asks, "What did he die from?"

"I think he died from a cerebral hemorrhage deep inside the brain."

Alan says, "I'll call his brothers."

Ten minutes later, Louis Rodriguez and Danny Johnson arrive. They are very upset.

Louis says, "Was his death caused by the car incident and head injury this past spring?"

Paul answers, "Yes, I think so."

Danny looks at Alan Sinclair. He says, "I'll miss him."

Arturus and I float away from the scene.

Arturus says, "You have to go back into the Bardo now. You'll be on your own."

The Bardo, Hell, Purgatory

The hell beasts, ghouls, ghosts and other creatures in the Bardo tear my soul apart. I may not have a physical body but my spiritual body is torn from limb to limb. The feeling is like having skin shredded from your body while your heart is ripped out. The pain and anguish are excruciating.

I am back in hell or purgatory or whatever it is. I pass by the evil sounds of Johnny Bizarro and the Bizarro Brothers Band. I finally arrive at the table of Pancho Villa. He is always glad to see me.

I ask Pancho, "I am not sure why we killed those people in Rumson, New Jersey."

"Remember, George the Bear ordered the killings. They were part of our mission. Those Europeans were planning World War III. By killing them the process is slowed down. Other more rational men can come to power. Those men were demons, they were sent by the Devil to wreak havoc on earth.

Then Pancho says, "I have a question for you Jaime. Do you remember where you were killed when we rode together a hundred years ago?"

"Yes, at the battle of Zacatecas."

"You always were a good and loyal soldier."

There is a reptilian smell in the air. The Devil comes into the place we inhabit. He laughs loudly at Pancho and me.

The Devil says, "Welcome back jerk-offs."

Pancho Villa looks the Devil in the eye and says, "Chinga Te, Tu Chingando Chinga."

END

ABOUT THE AUTHOR

Information about the author can be found at the following websites.

www.jamescage.net

http://jamescage.hubpages.com/

E-Books by James Cage

Back from the Bardo (original edition)
Sambalanga (screenplay)
Holding the Bricks (screenplay)
The Boareen Rife (science fiction)
The Last Marathon (essay)
Teniendo los Ladrillos (español)
Astral Andy y el Oso Divertido (español)
The Mind of Frank Rosseus
Back from the Bardo (second edition)

E-books can be located at Smashwords.com, Amazon.com, and other outlets.

23334814R00101

Made in the USA
San Bernardino, CA
15 August 2015